"You have exactly five minutes to say your piece."

Gabe could tell from the expression on Sara's face that she meant to send him packing the moment five minutes were up.

"I know my brother had his faults, but turning his back on his own child wasn't one of them. Blood kin is blood kin. We Coulters have always taken care of our own."

"Well, here's a news flash for you," she said. "I made the decision not to tell Billy about Ben because there wasn't any reason to tell Billy about Ben. It wasn't like Billy was father material."

This wasn't going as planned. In fact, nothing about his interactions with her had. He needed some way to show her that her son, *his nephew,* needed to know his Coulter heritage. Gabe pulled the check from his front shirt pocket, unfolded it and held it up for her to see. "Take Billy's insurance money. Use it to start a new life for yourself. But let Ben go back to Colorado with me. Let me give Ben the home and the legacy Billy would have."

She stared at the check as if it were a coiled rattlesnake ready to strike. Then she glared at Gabe. "You must be crazy if you think I'd trade my son for money."

Dear Reader,

In 1999 my dream came true. I sold my first romance to Harlequin Books. Now ten years later I'm thrilled to be back home with my first Harlequin Superromance novel.

Over the past decade I've written about single women looking for Mr. Right. I've written about housewives keeping hubby happy. But I've never had the chance to write about the kind of woman I was once–a single mom. Thanks to Harlequin Superromance, I've been given that opportunity.

I know exactly what it's like to have more month than money. I know the agony of worrying if you've made the right decisions. And I know how hard it is shouldering the responsibility alone. But I also know the joy of being a mom far outweighs any hardships we face along the way.

A Ranch Called Home is my tribute to the single mom. And my message is simple: regardless of your finances or the mistakes you make, you still possess the most precious gift we can give our children–a mother's everlasting and unconditional love.

Best always,

Candy Halliday

A RANCH CALLED HOME

Candy Halliday

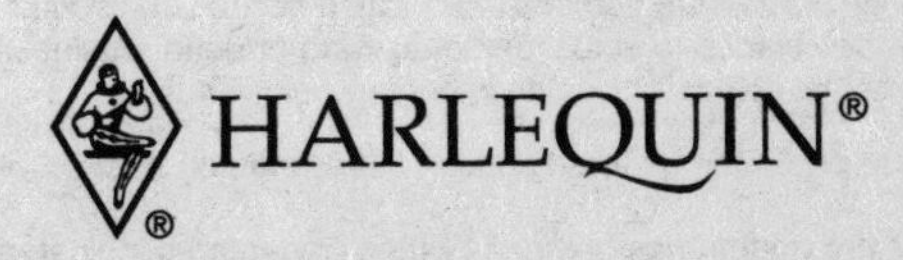

TORONTO • NEW YORK • LONDON
AMSTERDAM • PARIS • SYDNEY • HAMBURG
STOCKHOLM • ATHENS • TOKYO • MILAN • MADRID
PRAGUE • WARSAW • BUDAPEST • AUCKLAND

ISBN-13: 978-0-373-78320-5

A RANCH CALLED HOME

This edition published by arrangement with Harlequin Books S.A.

www.eHarlequin.com

Printed in U.S.A.

ABOUT THE AUTHOR

Candy Halliday embraced women's lib in the 60s, was a 70s single mom, married her Mr. Right in the 80s, became a proud grandmother in the 90s, and sold her first romance novel at fifty. Growing old gracefully has never been on Candy's agenda. And since sixty is the new fifty and chubby is the new thin, Candy claims life in her world is good. Candy's best advice: never put an age limit on your dreams.

Books by Candy Halliday

HARLEQUIN DUETS

58–LADY AND THE SCAMP
82–WINGING IT
103–ARE MEN FROM MARS?/VENUS, HOW COULD YOU?

This book is dedicated to my best friend
Lynda Tucker, an amazing single mom who has
always been there for me through the good times and
the bad. I love you, Tucker. Your friendship means
more than words could ever express.

Acknowledgments

Special thanks to my wonderful agent
Jenny Bent for putting up with me.

A million thanks to my fabulous editor
Wanda Ottewell for giving me the chance
to prove I can write traditional romance
as well as romantic comedy.

Thanks to author Emilie Rose, my fellow
romance sister, who keeps me pointed
in the proper writing direction.

Congrats to all my Duetter buddies as we celebrate
our tenth anniversary together in 2009.

And thanks always to my incredible,
supportive and loving family:
Blue, Shelli, Tracy, Quint and Caroline—
you guys rock!

CHAPTER ONE

GABE COULTER BOLTED upright in bed at the shrill ring of his bedside phone. When the person on the other end confirmed what Gabe had been waiting months to hear, he switched on his bedside light.

"And you're certain you found them?"

"I'm positive," the private detective said. "She and the kid are living in Conrad, Texas, a two-bit town just north of El Paso. She waits tables in a diner next door to a motel where they live. The boy stays in a back room at the diner while she works."

"She hasn't married?"

"Nah, she's still single," the detective said. "Still goes by the name Sara Watson. The kid's name is Ben."

"Ben," Gabe half whispered.

Finally, he had a name.

He raked a hand through his hair, slowly processing the information. Finding them hadn't been easy. The next step would be even harder.

"What do you want me to do now, Mr. Coulter?"

“Give me a second to get to my office,” Gabe said.

Grabbing his jeans from the bottom of the bed, Gabe pulled them on. With the phone still to his ear, he hurried downstairs in search of a pen and paper. He found what he needed on the massive mahogany desk that had served three generations of ranchers at the Crested-C.

What Gabe didn’t need was looking up to find that the late-Monday-night phone call had also awakened his foreman. The old man was standing in his office doorway, a worried expression on his gray-bearded face.

“I finally got a few photos of the woman and the boy,” the detective said. “But everything in Conrad is already closed for the night. I’ll have to drive back to El Paso before I can fax them to you.”

“That won’t be necessary,” Gabe said, jotting down the name and address of the diner. “I’ll leave as soon as I get my gear together. If I drive all night, I should be there in time to surprise her tomorrow.”

“That’s not a bad idea, Mr. Coulter,” the detective agreed. “She runs every time I pick up her trail. Conrad is nothing but a mud puddle in the middle of nowhere. It won’t take long before word gets around town that I was asking questions about her and the boy tonight.”

“You’ve earned that bonus we talked about,”

Gabe told the detective. "I'll be in touch as soon as I get back."

"Good luck," said the detective.

And Gabe knew he was going to need it.

He lowered himself onto the chair behind his desk, staring at the address he held in his hand. He purposely ignored the presence still looming in his office doorway. It should have been a subtle hint for Smitty to leave Gabe alone and go back to bed. But Smitty never had been good at doing what other people wanted.

"You just can't let sleeping dogs lie, can you, Gabe?"

Gabe and the old man traded scowls.

"Spare me the lecture, Smitty. I'm fully capable of making my own decisions."

"Well, you sure can't prove that by me." Smitty snorted. He pulled his suspenders up and over his stooped shoulders before he pointed a gnarled finger in Gabe's direction. "The search for that boy should have ended when your brother was killed, and you know it."

A muscle in Gabe's jaw clenched.

The pain of Billy's death was still as raw as the day of the accident. Images he usually kept at bay clicked through Gabe's mind like a horror film: Billy waving to the cheering crowd as he lowered himself onto the back of eighteen hundred pounds of raw muscle; cheers turning to terrified gasps when the angry bull reared; every bull rider's nightmare coming true as Billy fell backward into the stall; cowboys running from every direction trying to rescue their trampled hero.

A cold shiver passed straight through Gabe.

He shook it off and forced the memories into the shadows where they belonged. He only wished he could do the same with Smitty's damn opinions. But the old man had more than earned the right to speak his mind, and they both knew it.

Had it not been for Smitty, Gabe never would have been able to hang on to the ranch after his folks died. Smitty had stepped in as surrogate father when Gabe needed him most. Smitty had helped run the ranch, and he'd helped raise Billy. The old man just kept forgetting Gabe was thirty-three years old now, not the inexperienced kid he'd been fifteen years earlier when his parents died.

"Billy told you himself that gal never even told him she was pregnant," Smitty said, finally forcing the argument Gabe had known was coming from the day he took over the search for his brother's son. "She didn't want anything to do with Billy then. What makes you think she'll let you near the boy now?"

"There's a good chance the boy's mother won't let me near him," Gabe admitted. "But I wouldn't be much of a man if I conveniently forgot I have a nephew because my brother is dead."

"*Might* have a nephew," Smitty reminded him. "You don't even know if that boy belongs to Billy."

"Billy thought the boy was his," Gabe said. "Unless I find out otherwise, that's good enough for me."

"Mark my words, Gabe. You're borrowing trouble."

"Maybe so. But there's a five-year-old boy in Texas who could be my nephew. Trouble or not, I'm going to see him."

Smitty shook his head in disgust. "You know the type of woman you're dealing with, Gabe. You have her whole life story in a file in your top desk drawer."

"All the more reason to check on the boy."

"All the more reason to let the boy *go!*" Smitty shouted. He frowned at Gabe again. But he lowered his voice when he added, "You've worked hard holding on to this ranch. And for what? To let some one-night stand Billy met on the rodeo circuit lay claim to half the ranch your pa and your grandpa spent their whole lives building up?"

Gabe didn't answer.

He got up from his chair, walked across the room and took down the framed portrait of his parents on their wedding day. When he opened the wall safe hidden behind the picture, Smitty let out a weary sigh.

"Don't do this," Smitty said. "If you hand Billy's insurance money over thinking you'll be rid of the boy's mother, you're kidding yourself. She'll be holding her hand out for the rest of your life."

Gabe still didn't answer. He wrote out a check to Sara Watson for fifty thousand dollars and placed the checkbook back inside the wall safe. After he rehung his parent's picture, the old man was still blocking his path.

"I shouldn't be gone more than a few days," Gabe said, putting an end to any further discussion.

Defeated, Smitty finally stepped aside.

But as Gabe started up the stairs to pack, Smitty called out after him, "Watch your back, you hear me, Gabe? That little gal's liable to scratch your eyes out if you get within shouting distance of them."

Gabe threw a hand up to signal he'd heard the warning.

But by noon tomorrow, he intended to be in Texas.

If the boy did turn out to be his nephew, Billy's fifty thousand dollars in insurance money would be well spent if it meant bringing his brother's son home to Colorado where the boy belonged.

GABE PULLED his truck to a stop in front of a shabby diner called Dessie's at exactly ten minutes past noon on Tuesday, May twenty-ninth. The irony of the date wasn't wasted on Gabe. Had Billy lived, it would have been his brother's twenty-sixth birthday.

The fact that the motel beside the diner was nothing but a string of rundown buildings in an equally rundown town gave Gabe hope. Offering fifty thousand dollars to a woman stuck in a place like Conrad could be the big break he needed.

He grabbed his Stetson sitting on the bench seat beside him and jammed it onto his head. The second he stepped out of the truck, the unbearable Texas heat took his breath away. Why anyone would choose to live in such a dry, hot and desolate place was something Gabe would never understand. But then, he suspected most people wouldn't understand why he chose to endure the bitter cold mountain winters on the West Elk Slope in Colorado.

Different strokes for different folks, Gabe decided and nodded politely to the two old men sitting outside the diner beneath a faded awning. A small table and a checkerboard between them, these two Conrad citizens didn't appear to be affected by the sweltering heat at all.

"Dessie's is always packed for lunch," one of

the old men told him. "But the home cooking is worth the wait."

"Thanks for the tip," Gabe said, and opened the diner door.

The second he stepped inside, Gabe saw her.

She was on the flashy side just as he'd expected. Bleached-blond hair. Too much makeup. Her sexy figure more than emphasized by the tight-fitting uniform she wore.

He walked past her, heading to a booth in the back—the only empty seat in the place. By the time he slid into the booth and placed his Stetson on the seat beside him, she was busy taking orders from three men sitting at a table near the diner's front window.

Gabe watched as she openly flirted with each of the men, a come-on smile on her cherry-red painted lips. He smiled inwardly, knowing, if his gut instinct was correct, she'd hand the boy over the minute he flashed the money in her direction.

And thinking about the boy, Gabe took a quick look around the diner, surveying the situation. The detective had mentioned a back room. The best Gabe could tell, a sign pointing down a hallway to the restrooms was the most likely place for this room.

He'd give this Sara Watson a chance to let him see the boy first. If she refused, Gabe had already decided he was not leaving Texas without seeing the child who could very well be his nephew. Despite Smitty's doubts, he'd know if the boy belonged to Billy the second he saw him—Coulter genes were hard to hide.

She glanced in his direction and gave another come-on smile. "Be with you in a minute," she called out.

Gabe nodded.

He watched as she clipped the order she had just taken to a revolving wheel above an open window separating the diner from the kitchen. A skinny old woman with gray hair grabbed the order and pushed two plates back through the window at her. The blonde took the plates and placed them in front of a man and a woman sitting at the counter. Next, she walked to the register to take another customer's money.

"Give me just a few more minutes, honey," she called out to Gabe again, holding up a finger to signal she would be right back.

Don't worry, honey. *I'm not going anywhere,* Gabe thought as she disappeared down the hallway.

He'd been waiting over a year for this moment. He could wait a few minutes longer.

SARA PEEKED around the storage-room door and smiled when she saw her son sitting on the folding cot happily playing with his favorite toy—a plastic horse he'd named Thunder—and his constant companion. Being able to check on Ben every few minutes was a huge relief. In fact, Sara sometimes wondered if her guardian angel had been responsible for making her worn-out car break down in Conrad, Texas.

She and Ben had been shown nothing but kindness here.

She'd sold the car for parts when the mechanic at the town garage broke the news that the vehicle wasn't worth what it would take to fix it. The mechanic had also sent her to see Dessie McQueen, a woman in her sixties who had seen her own share of hard times.

Dessie owned the town's only diner and motel.

Calling Dessie a godsend would be an understatement.

She'd allowed Sara to work in the diner in exchange for a motel room and three meals a day for her and her son. And no money exchanged meant no payroll records to leave a paper trail behind. It had also been Dessie's idea to fix up the storage room so Sara wouldn't have to pay for child care for Ben.

"Keep your tips and get back on your feet," Dessie had told her. "Until you do, we'll keep the same arrangement."

Sara had intended to do just that.

What she hadn't intended was leaving Conrad so soon.

She glanced at the packed suitcases sitting beside Ben's cot and felt like crying. The detective she'd been eluding for over a year had somehow managed to track her down again. As soon as the busy lunch shift was over, Dessie would be driving Sara and Ben back to her hometown of Houston. She and Ben would stay with her best friend Annie Riley for a few days until Sara could figure out where to go next.

And it was only fair that Annie should take them in.

Annie, after all, had been responsible for the detective being on Sara's trail in the first place. Had Annie not run into her son's father, Billy Coulter never would have known about Ben.

Billy Coulter, Sara thought. *My first and* last *mistake.*

She and Annie had been working the concession stand at the rodeo the summer before their senior year in high school when Sara met Billy Coulter. The handsome rodeo star had filled her head with empty promises then had ridden off with her innocence and not so much as a backward glance.

Sara had intended to keep it that way.

But in less than a week after big-mouth Annie

told Billy he had a son, a private detective had arrived at Annie's apartment complex asking questions. Fearing a costly custody battle Sara couldn't afford, she'd taken Ben and left Houston before Billy could find them.

Then news of Billy's fatal accident at the World Champion Rodeo Finals in Las Vegas had been plastered all over the papers and the television for days. She'd assumed the search for them would end after Billy's death. But Sara really got worried when the detective tracked them down again in Fort Worth.

Someone was still searching for her son.

But she'd run forever if that's what it took.

She'd never let anyone take Ben away from her. Never.

GABE BRACED himself when the woman he'd come to proposition finally came around the corner and walked in his direction.

"What can I do you for, handsome?" she teased when she walked up to the table.

"That depends," Gabe said.

She leaned forward, her hands resting on the table. And whether Gabe was interested or not, he had a bird's-eye view of her more-than-ample breasts pressing against the thin fabric of her low-cut uniform.

She leaned even closer. "That depends on what, cowboy?"

"On whether your name is Sara Watson," Gabe said.

The blonde gasped and jumped back.

"Sara!" she yelled over her shoulder. "Run!"

Gabe looked past the blonde. He hadn't seen this waitress when he'd entered the diner. Staring back at him was someone who was anything *but* the type of woman he expected. Her face was scrubbed free of makeup and her dark hair was piled loosely on top of her head.

Beautiful—that's what she was.

And her dark brown eyes were now wide with fear.

She looked at him a second longer, turned and ran.

"Wait!" Gabe jumped up from the booth.

Every man in the diner stood when Gabe did.

"I don't want any trouble here," Gabe said, looking around at the frowning faces.

"Leave the same way you came in," a big guy near the front door said, "and there won't be any trouble here."

Gabe shook his head. "No. I'm not leaving until I talk to Sara Watson and her son."

"Wrong answer," the big guy said.

He took a threatening step in Gabe's direction.

CHAPTER TWO

AT FIRST, Sara thought she'd seen a ghost.

The family resemblance was that frightening.

Same sun-streaked hair. Same piercing blue eyes. Same determined, square-cut jaw. Whoever the man was, he was a Coulter. And Sara knew he was looking for the Coulter she was running to find now.

"Ben, come with me," she ordered, trying not to sound as frightened as she was when she hurried into the storage room.

Had it not been for the commotion going on in the dining room, Ben would have obeyed her. But raised voices and loud crashes were too much for any little boy to ignore. Before Sara could grab him, Ben jumped down from the cot and ran out with his toy horse under his arm.

Sara ran after him.

"Call the sheriff!" she called to Dessie as she hurried down the hallway past the kitchen.

"Sheriff Dillard's on his way," Dessie replied.

By the time Sara made it into the dining room,

tables were overturned and all of the customers were on their feet. In a panic, Sara pushed through the crowd.

"Ben!"

"Over here, Sara," someone called out.

Sara hurried toward two of the local men who were thankfully blocking Ben's path. The concerned looks on their faces told her the intruder was still in their midst. Sara had no sooner uttered a grateful thank-you to her son's protectors than someone else yelled, "Hit him again, Mack!"

Both men automatically turned back toward the action.

And Ben saw his opportunity to wiggle between them.

Sara's grab for the back of Ben's shirt came a second too late. Before she could stop him, her curious son darted into the center of the crowd. And when Sara pushed through after him, she found Ben standing above a man sprawled flat on his back.

"Are you hurt, mister?" Ben asked.

A hush fell, as if everyone awaited the guy's answer.

He finally sat up, bringing himself to eye level with the little towhead staring at him. Instinctively, Sara stepped forward and pushed Ben behind her. Still, Ben peeped around her apron, staring at the stranger with the same startling blue eyes that this man had himself.

"You must be Ben," he said, sticking his hand out. "I'm your Uncle Gabe."

"Wow," Ben said, stepping around Sara. He shook the hand he was being offered. "I've never had no uncles before."

"Nice horse you have there," he said.

"His name's Thunder," Ben said with pride.

"I like horses, too," he told Ben. "I have a lot of horses on my ranch in Colorado."

"Wow," Ben said again, turning around to look at Sara. "Did you hear that, Mom? Uncle Gabe has lots o' horses on his ranch in Col-dorado."

Several people chuckled over Ben's pronunciation.

But not Sara.

She placed her hand gently on Ben's shoulder, nudging her son away from the man who was threatening to steal her sanity. "Go back to your playroom now, Ben, and stay there until I come for you," Sara said sweetly.

The look she sent *Uncle Gabe* was anything *but* sweet.

How dare he introduce himself to Ben!

She looked at her son to find Ben's mouth puckered in a little-boy pout. "Go now, Ben," Sara repeated, and gave her son a gentle push.

"Okay, Mom," Ben finally said, but he sent a small wave in his uncle's direction. "Bye, Uncle Gabe."

Gabe pulled himself up and dusted himself off. "See you later, partner," he had the nerve to say.

Over my dead body! Sara vowed.

The people suddenly parted and Sheriff Dillard walked up beside her. Howard Dillard was a big man, in his early sixties, and extremely fit for his age. People in Conrad called him Mr. Clean, not only because of his sterling reputation but also because he resembled the TV commercial character.

Dillard removed his hat and blotted his bald head with his handkerchief. "Is this the guy causing all the trouble?"

"He's the one," Dessie called out from the kitchen.

Sara and everyone else nodded in agreement.

And Sara could only pray the ugly bruise forming on the stranger's left cheek had given him the clear message he was *not* welcome in Conrad.

He looked at Dillard and said, "My name is Gabe Coulter and I didn't come here to cause any trouble. I came to see my nephew."

Dillard purposely looked around at the damage.

"And I didn't start the fight," he added quickly. He pointed to one of the locals standing in the back of the diner. "That big guy started the fight."

Dillard looked over his shoulder. "Is that true, Mack? Did you start the fight?"

"No way, Sheriff," Mack said. "He took the first swing then I decked him."

Everyone looked back at Gabe.

"Forget it," he said, shaking his head. "It's obvious I'm outnumbered here. I'll pay for the damages."

"And what about the damage you did to my son?" Sara demanded, hands on her hips now. "How dare you waltz in here and inform my son you're his uncle without my permission. Don't you realize how confusing that could be for a five-year-old?"

"You tell him, Sara," someone in the crowd agreed.

He simply stood there, staring at her.

"I apologize," he finally said. "You're right. I shouldn't have introduced myself to Ben without your permission. But when I saw him, he looked so much like my brother when Billy was that age, that I..."

Sympathy pulled at Sara's heartstrings for a second.

But only for a second.

And Dessie definitely wasn't sympathetic over the mess the fight had made. She entered the room, drying her hands on her apron as she marched in their direction. When she stopped beside Sara, Dessie pushed a strand of gray hair off her forehead and looked over at the sheriff. "I want to press charges, Howard. Lock the boy up. Maybe if he spends the night in jail it will improve his manners."

Gabe laughed. "I can make my own bail, Sheriff."

Dillard frowned. "You want to bet on that, son?"

"No. I can already see where this is going. But I've told you I'll pay for the damages. And I've apologized for introducing myself to my nephew without his mother's permission." Gabe glanced at Sara for a second. "If she'd stop running from me long enough to hear me out, she'd know I only want what's best for the boy."

"Stop running from you?" Sheriff Dillard repeated. "Are you saying you've been stalking Sara?"

"Yes," Sara said. "He's been stalking me for over a year now."

"The hell I have," Gabe said. "I haven't been stalking her at all. I've only been trying to *talk* to her."

Sheriff Dillard turned to Sara. "Are you interested in anything this man has to say, Sara?"

"Not in a million years," Sara said, staring him down.

But she shouldn't have taken such a long look at him.

Despite the family resemblance, there was something about him that told Sara physical appearances were where the similarities between the two brothers ended. Billy had been loud and boisterous, with a fast line and a devil-may-care attitude. This man had an air of confidence about him that said he took life seriously. The determined expression on his face said he was used to getting what he wanted.

Everything about him spelled danger.

Tall. A hard, lean body. Exceptionally broad shoulders. He was all cowboy from his tight-fitting shirt and faded jeans, right down to the tip of his high-dollar boots.

And those eyes.

Penetrating.

Challenging.

A similar pair of blue eyes had led her down a treacherous path before. But Sara saw something she hadn't expected in this man's eyes. She'd seen genuine affection for Ben when Gabe met his nephew for the first time.

That realization scared Sara even more.

"You heard the lady," Sheriff Dillard said. "Sara isn't interested in anything you have to say. But because I'm a reasonable man, I'm going to give you a chance to avoid any jail time. You pay Dessie for the damages. Then you go back to wherever you came from. And you agree to leave the boy and his mother alone."

"No," Gabe said stubbornly. "Not until she hears me out."

He kept staring at her.

Sara glared at him.

"Well, Sara?" Sheriff Dillard said. "Are you willing to talk to him? Or do I lock him up?"

"Lock him up," Sara told the sheriff.

She wheeled around and left without a second thought. Sheriff Dillard would keep Gabe Coulter in jail for at least twenty-four hours—Dessie would see to it. By then, Sara and Ben would be long gone.

"Ah, come on, Sheriff," she heard Gabe say. "Are the handcuffs really necessary?"

Guilt washed over Sara for a second.

But only for a second.

She hated that he was going to jail, but he'd chosen his own fate. He'd found her. She'd told him she wasn't interested in anything he had to say. So he should have accepted her answer and gone back to Colorado the way Sheriff Dillard suggested.

Jail was Gabe Coulter's own fault—not hers.

With a clear conscience, Sara hurried down the hallway. She was going to find her son. Then she was going to get as far away as possible from another handsome Coulter who was threatening to turn her life upside down.

"WHERE'S UNCLE GABE?" Ben hopped off the cot when Sara entered the storage room.

Sara's heart sank.

She knew Ben was starved for male attention. Had she not watched more men than she could remember drift in and out of her mother's life, she might have been more receptive to dating after Ben was born. But having Ben get attached to someone only to have the guy eventually move on was not a chance Sara had ever been willing to risk.

Ben was *not* going to grow up the way she had.

But that was a lifetime ago, Sara reminded herself.

And she wasn't her mother.

Kneeling beside him, Sara pulled Ben to her chest for a fierce hug. She'd allowed her own fears to rob Ben of knowing his father, and she'd always regret that. She'd planned to avoid Billy only long enough to find a better job and get a decent place to live—something more suitable than the welfare-assisted housing project she'd been living in when Annie first told Billy about Ben. Then Sara would have contacted Billy on her terms—even agreed to let him meet Ben *after* she was positive no court of law could say she wasn't able to take care of Ben properly.

But Billy was dead now.

And Gabe Coulter had no claim on her son.

"Mom, you're squishing me."

Sara released him and forced a smile. "Your uncle Gabe had to go back to Colorado, sweetie."

The disappointment on his little face made Sara wince.

"But as soon as Dessie gets through serving lunch, you and I are going to go visit Aunt Annie," she said. "Won't that be fun?"

Ben nodded, but he didn't look convinced.

"You remember how much you like staying with Aunt Annie and her dog, Coco," Sara reminded him. "And remember how much fun you have going to the pool at Aunt Annie's apartment complex?"

Ben frowned. "But I wanted to see Uncle Gabe's horse."

"But sweetie," Sara said patiently, "Uncle Gabe didn't bring his horse. His horses are on his ranch in Colorado."

Ben's face brightened. "Can we go to Coldorado and see them?"

Thankfully, Sara was saved from an answer when Dessie walked in. She leaned over and whispered in Sara's ear, "Coulter's on his way to jail."

Then Dessie straightened and sent Ben a big smile. “Ready for lunch, little buddy? I fixed you a big hamburger with extra, extra cheese. Just the way you like them.”

The promise of a juicy cheeseburger sent Ben running.

As soon as Ben left, Dessie looked at Sara and said, “Before I take you to Houston, I think you should stop by the jail and talk to this Coulter man.”

“Absolutely not!”

“You heard him yourself, Sara. He isn’t going to stop chasing you until you talk to him.”

Sara’s chin lifted. “Then I’ll—”

“Keep running?”

Sara refused to answer.

“And what about when it’s time for Ben to start kindergarten in the fall? Are you going to spend the rest of your life dragging Ben from one town to another? From one school to another?”

“Don’t you think I’ve thought about that? That’s all I have thought about, Dessie. But this man wants more than just to talk to me. I could see it in his eyes. He wants Ben!”

“Maybe, maybe not,” Dessie said. “You won’t know for sure until you talk to him.”

Sara slumped onto the folding cot. “And what if I’m right?” She looked up at Dessie for an answer. "What if he wants Ben and he threatens to take him away from me?"

"Then you threaten him with a restraining order if he doesn't stop harassing you," Dessie said. "You're a good mother, Sara. Don't you ever doubt that."

"No, Dessie," Sara corrected, "I'm a struggling mother who can barely provide for Ben. All it takes is one call to Social Services. And I should know. That's how I ended up in the system."

"But there's one thing you have that your mother didn't," Dessie said.

Sara looked up again. "And what's that?"

"The courage to stand up and fight for your son," Dessie said. "You march over to the jail right now and you tell that cowboy he picked the wrong mother to mess with."

CHAPTER THREE

THE LAST PERSON Gabe expected to see again was the very person who walked up and stopped in front of his jail cell. Arms folded stubbornly across her chest, her pretty nose was held high in the air, and the expression on Sara's face was deadly serious.

"You have exactly five minutes to say what you came to say," she said with authority. "Then I want you out of our lives. If you ever come near us again, I'll get a restraining order against you."

So that's how she's going to play it.

He'd caught her off guard at the diner, and it scared her. She'd reappeared now to prove she was in complete control of the situation.

He rose slowly from the cot and took his time walking the short distance across the cell. He'd rehearsed the speech he planned to give his nephew's mother a thousand times. Now, all he could think about was Smitty's "she'll scratch your eyes out" warning. It made Gabe thankful for the iron bars separating them at the moment.

She glanced at her watch. "Four minutes and counting," she warned.

"I know my brother had his faults, but turning his back on his own child wasn't one of them. It isn't the Coulter way of doing things."

"Well, here's a news flash for you," she said. "I'm not interested in the *Coulter* way of doing things. I have my own way of doing things. And I made the decision not to tell Billy about Ben because there wasn't any reason to."

"He was Ben's father," Gabe reminded her. "He had the right to know he had a child."

She looked him straight in the eye. "I disagree. DNA doesn't give you the right to be a father. You *earn* the right to be a father. I was eighteen and stupid when I met your brother, but I wasn't too stupid to realize Billy wasn't father material when he didn't even consider me worth a goodbye when he left Houston."

"People make mistakes," Gabe said.

"True. But it doesn't really matter now, does it? Billy is..." She faltered for a second, unable to say the word.

"Anyway," she said, "I'm sorry about your brother. But as far as I'm concerned any connection Ben had with your family ended with Billy."

Gabe frowned. "And that's where I disagree.

Blood kin is blood kin. We Coulters have always taken care of our own."

He pulled the check from his shirt pocket, unfolded it and held it up for her to see.

"Take Billy's insurance money," Gabe urged. "Use it to start a new life for yourself. But let Ben come to Colorado with me. Let me give Ben the home and the heritage Billy would have given Ben if my brother had lived long enough to find Ben himself."

Her reaction, however, wasn't what he'd hoped for. She stared at the check as if it were a coiled rattlesnake ready to strike.

"We're done here," she said.

She whirled around and walked away.

"I didn't come here to play games," Gabe called after her. "You go ahead and get your restraining order. But I have five years' worth of information on how well you've been able to provide for Ben alone. I don't think you want me to use that information against you in court."

She marched back to his cell.

"Now you're threatening me?"

Gabe stepped back from the bars. She was so angry she was shaking. And the expression on her face said threatening to counteract her in court was the *wrong* thing to do.

"Take me to court," she challenged. "I dare

you. If I cared a flip about your money, I would have shown up on your doorstep a long time ago. But a court of law might have a different idea. Force the issue and you may end up selling your horses and your ranch and giving Ben half of the proceeds."

The slam of the door at the end of the corridor as Sara left punctuated her words.

"Dammit!" he cursed, feeling like a first-class jerk.

He never should have offered her the money. And he definitely shouldn't have threatened her just because she threatened him. He could see that now. But put a woman in his path, and he never had a clue what to do next.

That's why he'd never had a woman in his life—at least not a full-time woman. Women were too complicated. Too temperamental. Too damn hard to please.

He was a rancher, not some smooth-talking womanizer like Billy. The ranch had always come first with Gabe, always would. He had horses to train. Ranch hands who depended on him for their livelihood. He didn't have time for this kind of bullshit.

"Damn you, Billy," Gabe muttered.

He walked away from the bars and flopped down on the solitary cot, wondering yet again how two brothers could have possibly been so different. He'd always been the responsible one—Billy never once considered the consequences of his actions.

Just like with Sara Watson.

There was no doubt in Gabe's mind Billy had taken advantage of her being eighteen and innocent, just as she'd claimed. And Gabe certainly couldn't blame her for coming to the conclusion that Billy wasn't father material.

Still, Gabe would chase her forever if that's what it took.

Unlike Billy, Gabe took his promises seriously.

And one way or another he would take his nephew home.

"WELL?" Dessie asked when Sara stormed back into the lobby of the sheriff's office. "What did he say?"

"Just as I expected," Sara said, still fuming. "He offered me money for Ben. And when I refused to take his fifty thousand dollars, he threatened to take me to court."

"Fifty thousand dollars," Dessie repeated, her eyes wide in disbelief.

"It could have been fifty million dollars and it wouldn't have mattered to me," Sara said, pacing to work off her anger.

"True," Dessie agreed, "but if he has that kind

of money to throw around, Sara, he's a bigger threat to you than I thought."

Sara stopped. "What do you mean?"

"Money talks," Dessie said. "And big money means high-powered attorneys. I hate to say it, but you wouldn't stand a chance against this cowboy in court."

"What's this about court?"

Sara and Dessie both turned. Sheriff Dillard walked out of his office into the lobby.

"Sara was right, Howard," Dessie said. "Coulter wants Ben. When Sara wouldn't take his money, he threatened to take her to court."

"Well, I just got off the phone with the sheriff in Pitkin County, Colorado," Sheriff Dillard said.

Dessie looked over at Sara. "Howard ran a check on Coulter's license plate. The Coulter ranch is located near a town called Redstone."

"And the Crested-C Ranch is one of the largest family-owned quarter-horse ranches in the state," Dillard added. "Sheriff Carter not only knows our boy, but Gabe happens to be an old fishing buddy of the sheriff's. Carter said Gabe is one of the most respected men in his county."

"That's strike two against you, Sara," Dessie warned. "He has money *and* he has a good reputation."

"There's something else that might shed some

light on why he continued looking for you after his brother was killed," Sheriff Dillard said. "Gabe was at the rodeo when his brother was injured. And according to Carter, Billy made Gabe promise during the ambulance ride to the hospital that he would find his son and bring the boy home."

Sara shuddered, thinking about the news footage she'd seen on TV. She hadn't realized one of the men hovering over Billy immediately after the accident was his brother. And apparently neither had the media, because Sara knew that story would have been milked for all it was worth.

"I hate to say it, Sara, but that's strike three against you," Dessie said, shaking her head sadly. "There isn't a jury alive who would rule against a man trying to carry out his dead brother's last wish."

"Will you stop being so negative, Dessie," Sara scolded. "What happened to the 'march in there and tell him he's messed with the wrong mother' lecture you gave me earlier?"

Dessie ignored Sara and directed her question to the sheriff. "Is Coulter married?"

"Oh, please!" Sara said. "What does his marital status have to do with anything?"

"His marital status has everything to do with this situation," Dessie argued. "If Coulter doesn't have a wife, who would take care of Ben if he did manage to win custody?"

They both instantly looked at Dillard for the answer.

"No wife," Dillard said. "The sheriff described him as a loner, completely devoted to the ranch and his horses."

"Well?" Sara asked, looking at Dessie, then back to the sheriff. "No wife means one point for my side, right?"

"Not necessarily," Dillard said. "Carter said their folks were killed in an accident when Billy was in grade school and Gabe was still a teenager. Gabe stepped up to the plate, took over the ranch, and raised Billy himself."

"And we all know how well that worked out," Dessie snipped.

"Now, Dessie," Sheriff Dillard said. "I hate to come to the man's defense, but a bull killed his brother. Not a lousy upbringing."

"Don't be so sure about that." Dessie snorted. "Coulter intends to raise Ben on a ranch with a bunch of rough and tough cowboys, the same way he raised his brother. If you ask me, that's too much testosterone for anyone's own good."

Sheriff Dillard let out a loud groan. "Can we please not turn this into a man-versus-woman thing?"

"Oh, hell, Howard," Dessie grumbled. "It's been a man-versus-woman thing since the beginning of time." She grabbed Sara by the arm. "Come on, Sara. We're wasting time talking to this old coot."

Sheriff Dillard immediately stepped in front of them.

"Stop right here, Dessie. I've known you too many years not to recognize that look on your face. You're up to something. And when you're up to something, it always means trouble for me."

Dessie pushed past him but said over her shoulder, "I'm depending on you to keep that boy locked up until tomorrow, Howard. And if you intend to be reelected next term you'll do your job."

With that said, Dessie marched Sara out the door.

GABE STOOD when he heard the door at the end of the hallway open. He was hopeful Sara Watson had thought things over during the past three hours, and had finally decided to reconsider his offer. Fifty thousand dollars, after all, was a lot of money for anyone to throw away on foolish pride.

His hope evaporated when the sheriff approached the cell. In typical lawman stance, both hands were at Dillard's waist, feet planted firmly apart.

He frowned at Gabe and said, "Your first mistake was offering Sara money in exchange for the boy."

Gabe didn't even bother to argue.

He'd already figured that much out for himself.

"Your second mistake," the sheriff said, "was threatening to take Sara to court."

"Well, what did you expect me to do?" Gabe asked. "She threatened me first with a restraining order."

"Do you really blame her?" Dillard asked. "You admitted you've been chasing her all across Texas for over a year now."

Gabe frowned. "I told you. I only wanted to talk to her."

"And it never crossed your mind the only reason she kept running was because you were chasing her?"

"Bullshit," Gabe said. "She kept running because she can barely keep a roof over her son's head."

"And you never considered offering Sara the money so she *would* be able to keep a roof over Ben's head?"

"This isn't about just keeping a roof over his head," Gabe said. "This is about his heritage and his future. Half of the Crested-C Ranch belongs to Ben now. And one day I hope he'll be the fourth generation to run it. But that isn't going to happen unless Ben grows up on his own land and the ranch actually means something to him."

"Then why didn't you tell Sara that instead of flashing your money in her face?"

"I didn't think it would make any difference to her."

"You don't have much experience in dealing with women, do you, son?"

Gabe sent him a warning look. "I'm in no mood for an education on dealing with women, Sheriff."

"That's too bad," Dillard said, "because your threats just put Ben and Sara in danger."

"And what's that supposed to mean?"

"Desperate people do desperate things," Dillard said. "After Sara left I sent my deputy over to the diner to keep an eye on her. I found out a few minutes ago she's taking the boy to Mexico."

"Mexico?"

"Dessie has a niece who runs a resort in Juarez just across the border from El Paso," Dillard said. "I'm sure that's where Sara will go. But do I need to draw a picture for you? Juarez is a dangerous place. Mexico's underground prostitution is big business in Juarez. And Sara and Ben would both bring top dollar."

Fear sucker punched Gabe in the stomach.

He shook the iron door in front of him.

"Then let me out of here, Sheriff! Help me stop her."

"Not so fast," Dillard said. "First, you tell me how committed you really are to your nephew."

"I'm here, aren't I?" Dammit! Gabe didn't have

time for stupid questions. Not with a dozen horrible scenarios already running through his mind.

"But are you here for the right reasons? I did a little checking on you, Coulter. I talked to your old pal Sheriff Carter. So look me in the eye and tell me the truth. Are you willing to do whatever it takes to give Ben the chance to grow up on his own land? Or are you really just trying to keep a half-assed promise you made to your dead brother?"

For the second time that day, Gabe was thankful for the iron bars in front of him. Had it not been for those bars—and the fact Dillard was thirty years his senior—Conrad's sheriff would have found himself flat on his back, compliments of Gabe's own fist.

But Gabe managed to reel in his anger. And he met Dillard's gaze with a deadly calm stare. "A man is only as good as his word, and there's never been anything half-assed about mine. I'll do whatever it takes to give Ben the chance to grow up on his own land."

Before Dillard could comment, a loud squawk from the radio on his hip prevented his answer. He pulled the radio from its clip and clicked the button. "Go ahead, Joe."

"They're on the move, Sheriff."

"Ten-four," Dillard told his deputy. He clipped the radio back on his belt before he pulled a key ring from his pocket. "I'm going to take a chance on you, Coulter, and let you prove how good your word really is."

"You won't regret it, Sheriff," Gabe promised, motioning for Dillard to hurry and open the door.

"But under one condition."

"Name it."

"If we stop Sara, you'll let *me* do the talking."

"Agreed," Gabe said, and he meant it.

He'd only make things worse.

CHAPTER FOUR

SARA BIT DOWN HARD on her lower lip when she saw the sign: Come Back to Conrad Again Soon. Lately she'd thought less and less about leaving Conrad and more and more about staying.

In fact, just last week she'd found a small furnished house for rent within walking distance of the diner. In a few weeks she would have had enough money saved to place a rent deposit on the house. Her nightly prayers had all been the same: the search for them would end and she and Ben could stop running and live a normal life.

But answered prayers were scarce in Sara's life. She should have gotten used to that by now.

"Don't look so worried," Dessie said, glancing over at Sara from behind the wheel of the dusty station wagon now headed for the border. "I know you've always considered Mexico your last resort, but aren't you glad I pushed you into getting your passports?"

Sara nodded, but only halfheartedly.

The thought had already crossed her mind that applying for their passports was probably responsible for the detective finding them again. But there was no point in mentioning that possibility to Dessie and making her feel guilty about it. What was done was done.

Still, Mexico *had* always been Sara's last resort.

She didn't like the thought of living in Mexico. And she certainly didn't like imposing on a stranger to take them in. Even if Dessie's niece was willing to give her a job at the resort and a place to stay, Sara still didn't like being put in the position to rely on anyone's charity.

She'd been a charity case her whole life.

And she'd hated every minute of it.

"Just think of this as a summer vacation," Dessie chirped with far more enthusiasm than Sara could muster. "As soon as Coulter knows you're in Mexico, he'll give up and stop following you, I'm sure of it. By the end of the summer, you and Ben can come back to Conrad and pick up your lives where you left off."

"I hope you're right," Sara said with a sigh.

"Of course I'm right," Dessie said with confidence.

But Sara wasn't so sure.

So many questions kept running through her mind. What if Gabe didn't give up? And what if those high-powered attorneys Dessie had mentioned earlier were able to extradite them from Mexico? Even worse, what if she and Ben remained stuck in Mexico indefinitely, trying to wait Gabe out?

Maybe, Sara decided, she should stopping running. Maybe she should stay in the States and take her chances in court. Fight for her rights. Prove to Gabe Coulter that she didn't intend to run from him for the rest of her life.

Her better judgment told her to turn around.

But before Sara could relay that message to Dessie, the high-pitched scream of a siren jerked Sara's head around.

"Why, that's Howard Dillard!" came Dessie's surprised cry when she looked in her rearview mirror.

Sara kept staring at the flashing blue light. "What do you think he wants?"

"I can't imagine," Dessie said. "But there's a rest area up ahead. We'd better pull over and find out."

Dessie pulled into the rest area a few minutes later, the patrol car right behind her. By the time the station wagon rolled to a stop, Ben had his seat belt unbuckled and was already climbing out of the booster seat he hated. Standing up in the backseat, he waved out the back window when two men got out of the cruiser and walked in their direction.

"It's Uncle Gabe!" Ben yelled, and bolted from the car.

"Ben!" Sara yelled.

She jumped out of the car after him.

But Sara froze when she saw Gabe bend down to scoop Ben up. Sara wasn't sure what worried her most—Ben looking so happy, or Sheriff Dillard looking so perturbed.

When they got close enough for her to snatch Ben away from Gabe, Sara wasted no time reaching for her son. Her gaze locked briefly with Gabe's, but he handed Ben over without an argument.

Dessie, on the other hand, didn't waste any time stepping in front of Sara. "What's going on, Howard?" she demanded, looking Gabe up and down. "And what's *he* doing out of jail?"

"Now, Dessie," Dillard said, "let's all calm down and take a seat." He pointed to a shaded picnic table a few yards away. "Nothing good ever comes from a hasty decision. Before Sara crosses the border, I want her to know she has another option."

"What other option?" Dessie was quick to ask.

Dillard nodded toward the picnic table again. "Like I said, Dessie, let's all sit down like reasonable adults and I'll tell you."

The sheriff headed for the picnic table.

So did Gabe and Dessie.

Sara first walked to the station wagon with Ben to retrieve his toy. She pointed to a water fountain several yards from the picnic table—far enough away that Ben couldn't overhear the conversation.

"Why don't you take Thunder over to that water fountain so you can both get a cool drink?" Sara told him, knowing her son would play in the water for as long as she would let him.

Ben made a beeline for the fountain.

And Sara headed for the picnic table. Ben's instant bond with his uncle had shaken her more than she wanted to admit. But she'd already made the decision that she was not going to Mexico.

She was going to stop running and fight for her son.

Mexico might come later.

If she lost custody in court.

GABE SAT UP a little straighter when Sara approached the picnic table. She refused to take a seat herself; instead she stood at the end of the table proud and erect.

He kept his word and waited for the sheriff to do the talking, but he couldn't keep his gaze from wandering where it shouldn't. She was gorgeous; no doubt about that. Curvy in all the right places. A face that would make angels in heaven weep with pure envy.

But she also had a feisty streak.

He'd seen that back at the jail.

And the way she scowled now made Gabe doubt that anything the sheriff could say was going to change her mind.

"What we have here," Sheriff Dillard said, "are two people concerned about Ben's welfare." He looked at Sara, then at Gabe. "Can we all at least agree with that statement?"

"No," she said, staring straight at Gabe. "I don't call threatening to take a child away from his mother being concerned about Ben's welfare."

Gabe felt the heat creep up the back of his neck.

He averted his eyes to his Stetson lying on the table in front of him. A random thought crossed his mind: the good guys always wore white hats. His hat was white. And he was trying to be the good guy in this situation.

But was he really the good guy?

Part of what Sara said was true. He hadn't only been thinking about what was best for Ben. Gabe had been thinking about what he wanted. *And* he'd been determined to keep the promise he'd made to his brother.

"Let's forget about court and custody battles, and move on to the solution I think I've found to this problem," Sheriff Dillard said. "Gabe, you told me earlier that Ben would be the fourth generation of Coulters to run the Crested-C Ranch. Is that correct?"

"Yes."

"But," Dillard said, "you also told me that the main reason you want Ben to go to Colorado is because the ranch isn't going to mean anything to Ben unless he grows up on the land. Is that also correct?"

"Yes," Gabe said, and he looked straight at Sara. "And I want to apologize to you, Sara, for not making myself clear back at the jail when I—"

"Move on," she snapped.

Women! Gabe thought. He'd sooner deal with a thousand-pound grizzly.

"Okay, Sara, let's move on," Sheriff Dillard agreed. "Ben's best interest will always be your first concern. Right?"

She nodded curtly.

"And that brings us to the other option I want both of you to consider," Dillard said. "The only logical way to settle this problem is with a compromise. Let Ben go to Colorado with Gabe and live on his own land, Sara. But you go with them."

She laughed.

That old bastard tricked me! was Gabe's first thought.

There hadn't been a woman on the Crested-C since his mother died. And if he brought a woman home now there would definitely be hell to pay. Smitty, the old grouch, had run off every cleaning lady Gabe had tried to bring in over the past fifteen years.

And what about his ranch hands? Many of them had only known the Crested-C as an all-man's world and that's the way they liked it. No need for social graces. No need to wipe your feet, or watch your language. Gabe would have a damn mutiny on his hands if he brought a woman home.

"If that's your idea of an option," she said, "forget it. I'm not interested."

Gabe breathed a sigh of relief.

Dillard banged his fist hard on the table.

Sara jumped.

So did Gabe.

"I'm not talking about what interests either of you!" Dillard boomed. "I'm talking about Ben's best interest. The boy needs a family, and he has one. He has a mother and he has an uncle. Instead of playing hide-and-seek all over the state of Texas, or battling it out in court, the two of you need to put your selfish issues aside and do what's best for Ben."

Gabe squirmed. He'd boasted earlier that he'd do whatever it took for Ben to live on the Crested-C. That a man was only as good as his word. That his word had never been half-assed.

Dillard was putting those assertions to the test.

And Gabe knew it.

Now it was time to stand up and be the man he claimed to be. Or, go ahead and admit his word was only half-assed, just as Dillard had originally accused.

He chanced another glance in Sara's direction.

She was staring right at him.

Gabe quickly looked away.

He didn't like her accusing glare—or what she'd said about taking Ben away from his mother not being in Ben's best interest. It brought back memories Gabe thought he'd buried long ago.

Unsettling memories.

Memories that cut open wounds that even time could never heal completely.

"I CAN'T BELIEVE I'm saying this, but for once I have to agree with Howard," Dessie said. "I'm sorry, Sara, but this could be a new beginning for you and for Ben. You could finally be a full-time mother. And Ben could grow up in one place, put down roots."

Sara couldn't believe what she was hearing. Dessie was supposed to be her ally.

"You can't be serious!" Sara gasped.

"I am," Dessie said. "If you and Gabe battle it out in court, Ben loses. Either he loses his heritage or he loses his mother. I say Ben deserves both."

Sara put her hands on her hips. "And you really expect me to take Ben to Colorado to live with a total stranger?"

"I'm not a total stranger. I'm Ben's uncle."

Sara shot him a mean look. "I wasn't talking to you."

"I realize that," he said. "But according to Sheriff Dillard, you were on your way to Mexico to live with a total stranger. I'm not sure I see the difference."

Sara's cheeks flushed crimson at the truth.

"He's right, Sara," Dessie said. "At least he's Ben's uncle."

How dare my friends take sides with him?

But *shocked* didn't cover her reaction when Gabe stood and held his hand out in her direction.

"I'm willing if you are, Sara," he said. "Come to Colorado with me and live on the ranch. For Ben's sake."

For Ben's sake.

Everyone was talking about what was best for Ben. But she was being backed into a corner.

And Sara didn't like it!

"For Ben's sake," Sara said, trying to keep the quiver out of her voice, "I'm going to pretend we never had this conversation."

She refused to shake Gabe's hand.

And she was trying *so* very hard not to cry. Her

friends siding against her threatened to pop the cork on a lifetime of bottled-up hurt. Instead of wallowing, Sara let her anger loose.

"Shame on all of you. How dare any of you act like you know better than I do what's best for Ben." She jammed a finger against her chest. "I happen to be a victim of other people deciding what was in my best interest. And do you know how that turned out? By the time I was eighteen I'd lived in four different foster homes. The houses were all nice enough. And the foster families were all pillars of the community. But it didn't make one bit of difference! I was always the outcast. And that's the same way Ben and I would be treated if we moved to Colorado to live on a ranch with his dead father's brother."

Sheriff Dillard started to say something, but Sara silenced him with one look.

"And don't anyone try to tell me that isn't true," she said. "I would always be the unmarried woman living with some man. *Respectable* women in town would whisper about me behind their hands. And Ben would get in fights on the playground over the ugly things other kids said about his mother. I lived that life. And I won't have Ben living it, too. So don't any of you *dare* try to tell me what's best for my son again."

"Oh, Sara, honey," Dessie said, reaching for Sara's hand.

Sara jerked her hand away.

She pushed her hair carefully back into place.

Once she'd regained her composure, Sara turned to Dessie and said, "I'm going to get Ben now. We'll be waiting for you in the station wagon."

Then she looked straight at Gabe. "If you want to file custody papers, Ben and I won't be hard to find this time. I'm tired of running from you. We're staying in Conrad."

Sara expected a comeback, but he didn't say a word.

He just kept standing there, a blank look on his face.

Exasperated, Sara stomped off.

"MARRY ME," Gabe blurted.

The minute he said it, he knew it was the right thing to do. He'd asked Billy once what he intended to do if he did find the boy and his mother.

"I'm going to do the same thing you would do if you were in this situation," Billy had said. "I'm going to ask her to marry me. And if she accepts, I'm going to bring her home and provide the best life I can for her and my son."

Gabe had been proud of Billy's answer.

But it had taken Sara's outburst before Gabe realized she was right on target about how she and Ben would be received in his small hometown if she lived at his ranch, no commitment between them. That's when Gabe had felt his brother's hand on his back, pushing him to finish what Billy couldn't.

Sara's spine was stiff, her fists still clenched in anger over a lifetime of other people pushing her around. He had a file filled with information on the lousy cards life had dealt her: no father in the picture; a mother arrested more than once for drugs and prostitution. The file was filled with details of a dozen different reasons why Sara Watson should have turned out to be the type of person Gabe assumed she was before he met her.

But they were words on paper, nothing more.

And Gabe was ashamed of himself.

He was ashamed for assuming she would hand over her son for money. And he was ashamed for making her such a thoughtless offer in the first place.

She slowly turned around. "*Marry* you? That's absurd and you know it."

"Maybe," Gabe agreed. "I'm sure you aren't interested in having a husband any more than I'm interested in having a wife. But this is about Ben. We'd be an official family if we married and made it legal. No whispers behind your back. No fights on the playground. No reason to be treated like outcasts."

Gabe couldn't quite decipher the expression on her face. Outright rage that he'd suggested marriage? Or sheer amusement over his unexpected proposal? Maybe a little of both.

"Why the sudden change of heart?" she demanded. "A few hours ago you were threatening to take me to court. And now you're going to insult me by suggesting we should get married and become an *official* family?"

Gabe knew he had one chance to say the right thing.

So he told the truth.

"I was wrong. I convinced myself Ben would be better off living on the ranch with me. That I could give him everything you couldn't. But I'd forgotten the nights Billy cried himself to sleep after our parents died because he missed our mother. I'd never do that to Ben. I realize that now."

SARA BLINKED BACK tears.

He looked so sad standing there, clutching the brim of his Stetson, the look on his face so solemn. This was her first glimpse of who this man was. Maybe he wasn't the enemy after all.

They were each aware of the sacrifice they'd have to make.

Both knew all of the reasons it wouldn't work.

Still, Sara was forced to face some cold, hard facts about her own contribution to her son's future. She had no home to give Ben. No promise of one day running his own ranch. And she certainly didn't have a proud family heritage dating back three generations to pass down to her son.

In truth, it was a daily struggle to make ends meet. Living paycheck to paycheck, always having more month than money and struggling to provide the bare necessities were the only things she'd probably ever be able to offer Ben on her own.

What would Ben choose if he were old enough to make the decision himself? Would Ben choose a ranch and his heritage? Or would he choose a mother's unconditional love? Most likely, Ben would choose both.

She would lay down her life for her son, without a second thought.

In comparison, marrying her son's uncle seemed like an easy choice—as long as she didn't stop to think about the consequences. Ben had already adopted Gabe as his immediate hero. She knew it was selfish, but she couldn't keep from wondering where that would ultimately leave her if she did accept Gabe's proposal for Ben's sake.

In the background, Sara suspected.

Married to a man in name only.

And possibly losing all influence over her son.

Was she really willing to risk Ben growing up with a bunch of rowdy cowboys who flirted with danger for sport? Could she really chance Ben following in Billy's footsteps and embracing the dangerous life of a rodeo star?

Yet in all fairness, Sara knew there were other dangers just as serious she'd have to steer Ben away from regardless of where he grew up. Ben falling in with the wrong crowd for one thing—a real threat for any boy who had no strong male influence in his life—and there would be enormous peer pressure as Ben grew older. Would she be able to keep Ben pointed in the right direction if her economic status forced them to live in less than desirable circumstances? Sara knew all too well that poverty often walked hand in hand with drugs and crime.

"Six months," Gabe said. "That's all I'm asking. Give us six months to see if we can live together on the ranch as a family. If things aren't working out at the end of that time, I'll have the marriage annulled. You and Ben can leave and you have my word I'll never bother you again."

Still, Sara remained speechless.

She felt addled, in a daze, completely unable to function—until a small tug on the hem of her uniform snapped her out of it. Ben stood behind her, Thunder under his arm, and sopping wet from head-to-toe.

"Can we, Mom, please?" he begged. "Can we

go live on Uncle Gabe's ranch and be a family just like Uncle Gabe said?"

Sara knelt and cupped his sweet, innocent face in both of her hands. "I'm sorry, Ben," she tried to explain, "becoming a family isn't that simple."

"But why, Mom?"

It was her son's favorite question.

And this time, Sara didn't have an answer.

CHAPTER FIVE

"I NOW PRONOUNCE you husband and wife," the justice of the peace said. He sent Gabe a wink before he added, "You may now kiss the bride."

Sara held her breath when Gabe moved forward. She let it out again when he bent down for Ben who'd been standing between them during the quickie ceremony.

Hoisting Ben up, Gabe winked back at the justice of the peace and said, "I think I'll let my best man have the honor of kissing the bride today."

Ben placed a noisy kiss on the side of Sara's cheek and rewarded her with a big smile.

"Are we a family now?"

Sara struggled for an answer.

But Gabe smiled and said, "Yes, Ben, we're a family now."

And that was that. They were a family now—even though Sara had claimed it wasn't that simple. No pomp and circumstance. No fancy wedding dress. And no husband vowing to love her forever.

Not the wedding of Sara's little-girl dreams.

"You made the right decision, Sara," Dessie said as they both watched Gabe and Ben walk toward Sheriff Dillard, who had filled in as the other witness for the ceremony.

Sara nodded absently.

From Tuesday forward, the week had gone by in such a blur she'd wondered if she were trapped in some bizarre dream. All she remembered clearly was that she'd been walking toward the rest area parking lot with Ben thinking that everything she owned was packed in the two ratty suitcases stored in the back of Dessie's station wagon.

She had no home to offer Ben.

No heritage.

And very little security.

That's when she'd marched to where Gabe stood. And that's when she'd agreed to give him the six months he asked for. He was offering Ben everything she couldn't—including giving her the opportunity to be a full-time mother to her son.

Only a fool would have turned down such an offer.

Even if it only lasted for the next six months.

Sheriff Dillard and Gabe had taken care of everything else. They'd arranged for the marriage license. And they'd arranged for the ceremony to take place on the first day of June, at precisely eleven o'clock in the morning, by the local justice of the peace in Sheriff Dillard's office.

She, on the other hand, had spent the next two days training the new girl Dessie had hired at the diner, and happily pretending her whole life wasn't going to change forever when Friday morning arrived.

"Mom!" Ben exclaimed, running toward her. "It's time to go cut our cake. Hurry."

He darted off before Sara could respond.

"You shouldn't have gone to the trouble of having a reception for us, Dessie," Sara said. "But I really appreciate you doing that."

"It's nothing fancy," Dessie said. She put her arm around Sara's shoulder and gave her a supportive squeeze. "But you've made a lot of good friends in Conrad. It seemed a shame not to give everyone the chance to say goodbye to you and Ben."

"Mom!" Ben yelled again. "Let's cut the cake."

"Mercy," Dessie said, laughing. "Let's go cut your wedding cake before that boy has a conniption fit."

Sara took a deep breath.

Gabe was waiting for her by the door with Ben.

But as she walked in their direction a cynical thought crossed Sara's mind: *At least we have cake.*

HAD ANYONE TOLD HIM he would go back to Colorado with his nephew *and* a wife, Gabe would have called that person a liar. But as Sara approached, Gabe knew uniting Ben's family instead of selfishly tearing it apart was the only responsible thing to do in this situation.

Responsibility, he could handle.

He'd provide Ben and Sara with a good home and a good life for as long as they were willing to stay on the Crested-C. They'd never want for anything under his care. And he would go back to running the ranch and keeping things in order, the same way he'd always done.

The difficult part would be not letting himself get too attached to Ben. He'd learned the unbearable heartbreak that came from losing people you cared about. He'd lost his parents, first. Then, Billy. And Gabe knew there was a good possibility he'd lose Ben at the end of six months.

But at least he'd kept his promise.

Ben was going home.

Gabe opened the door for Sara when she walked up beside them. The faint scent of her perfume mocked him for a moment as she exited the sheriff's office.

Sara wouldn't be an easy woman to ignore.

Just watching her unsettled Gabe.

She took Ben's hand and started across the street to the diner, and Gabe couldn't help but think that the pale blue dress she wore emphasized her tiny waist. His gaze drifted back to her dark hair—pulled up on top of her head again today, the only way he'd ever seen her wear it. It wasn't the first time he'd wondered how far down her back those silky strands would fall.

And thoughts like those were ones he couldn't afford.

That's why he'd laid all his cards right out on the table when he'd taken Sara and Ben to dinner the previous evening. He'd made sure Sara knew a friendship was all he'd ever want between them.

She'd agreed so fast, it actually bruised his ego.

But Gabe knew being realistic about their new living arrangement was a key factor if the family they'd created was going to be a success. He'd wanted to make sure Sara had no unattainable expectations from him, just as he had no unattainable expectations from Sara.

Their only focus would be Ben.

Just as it should be.

Sara had surprised him, however, by stating that she had no intention of being anyone's charity case. Unless he needed her help on the ranch she planned to find employment in Redstone so she could pay for her own room and board.

He'd nixed her idea of getting a job.

And he'd assured Sara she'd have her work cut out for her on the ranch. Taking care of the house and cooking three meals a day for him and his six full-time ranch hands wasn't going to be an easy task.

She hadn't even batted an eye. And that gave Gabe hope things might work out.

He and Sara would both be too busy to worry about some silly piece of paper that legally pronounced them husband and wife. He'd tend to the ranch. She'd tend to the house and the cooking. And they'd both tend to Ben.

No problem, Gabe thought with confidence.

Sara picked that exact moment to glance over her shoulder at him. It was only one look. And an innocent one at that. But Gabe suddenly got the feeling he could be in trouble.

"YOU TAKE good care of Ben and Sara," Dessie told Gabe as she and Sheriff Dillard escorted the new family to the diner's door after the reception. "In Texas we can still round up a posse in the blink of an eye."

"I'll keep that in mind," Gabe said.

Sara reached out and gave Dessie one last hug. "I can never thank you for all you've done for me."

"Oh, stop, before you make me cry," Dessie fussed. "Just remember. If things don't work out in Colorado, you always have a home waiting for you here in Conrad."

"I won't forget that," Sara promised.

Ben ran ahead to the white extended-cab pickup parked directly out front. On his tiptoes, Ben reached up and touched the fancy gold shield stenciled on the door. The words *Crested-C Ranch* were written in bold black letters inside the gold emblem.

"Can this *C* belong to me, Uncle Gabe?" Ben asked.

Ben pointed to the first letter of the word *Crested* and Sara knew her son was referring to the conversation he'd had with his uncle at dinner the previous evening. It still amazed her at how well Gabe had been able to explain things in terms simple enough for a five-year-old to understand.

"Your dad's in heaven now," he'd told Ben, "but he sent me to find you and your mom and bring you home."

Gabe had also told Ben his last name was going to be Coulter—a change Sara agreed to allow only after Gabe assured her he wasn't talking adoption, just the legal formality of changing Ben's last name. "The *C* will stand for you and me," Gabe had explained to Ben. "Gabe Coulter and Ben Coulter. The two owners of the Crested-C Ranch."

That conversation was the reason behind her son's question now. Ben obviously wanted to pick his own *C*.

"You can have either *C* you want, Ben," Gabe

said, ruffling her son's blond hair. "It doesn't matter to me."

"I want the *first C*," Ben said with a big grin.

"Okay, Mr. First *C*—" Gabe tickled Ben "—up and into the truck now. We're burning daylight, and we have a long way to go."

Ben was still giggling when Gabe opened the truck door and helped him climb into his booster seat in the backseat of the truck. Sara had headed for the passenger side when Ben asked his uncle another question.

"Are we going home to Col-dorado now, Uncle Gabe?"

"Yes," Gabe said. "We're going home to Colorado now."

Reality smacked Sara square in the face. She'd been lulled into a false security over the past few days with everyone assuring her she'd made the right decision. Even the ceremony and the reception had seemed surreal—as if she were only a bystander in someone else's life.

But this was *her* life.

This was her future for the next six months.

Oh. My. God! What have I done?

Her answer came when her new husband suddenly appeared at her side, extending his hand to help her step onto the running board and into the truck. Then they were on their way to the

Crested-C Ranch. A ranch where the *C* stood for Coulter. And where her son would be part owner of land that had been in the Coulter family for three generations.

Sara bit down hard on her lower lip to stop the trembling as she swallowed past the lump in her throat. She averted her gaze to the scenery beyond the passenger window. But if Gabe noticed she was in the middle of a major panic attack, he didn't let on. Instead, he fielded the questions Ben fired from the backseat.

She soon learned that there were 15,000 acres to the Crested-C Ranch. And that part of the property ran along the Crystal River, named such because the melting snow from the high mountain ranges left the water so clear you could see all the way to the bottom.

She learned that Redstone was nicknamed "The Ruby of the Rockies" and was founded in 1901 by a wealthy coal baron who built a forty-two-room castle for his wife, who was actually a real Swedish countess. When Gabe said touring Redstone Castle was the town's main tourist attraction and that you could take sleigh rides around the property in the winter, the idea of a sleigh ride had Ben clapping with glee.

But when Ben asked if he could ride a horse as soon as he got to the ranch, Gabe showed Ben the deep scar on his right hand that was the result of an argument he'd had with a strong-willed stallion when he wasn't much older than Ben was now. "And that's why you won't be permitted to go near the horses unless an adult is with you," Gabe had told Ben.

Although Sara fully approved of that rule, she remained silent on the issue. Just as she remained silent when Gabe informed Ben a border collie named Bess had a new litter of puppies. A puppy was something Ben had always wanted, and something Sara had never been able to give him. She'd had enough trouble trying to feed the two of them, much less a pet. Gabe also warned Ben that the barn cats were wild and would scratch you if you tried to pet them.

"I've never liked cats much," Ben said.

In fact, Gabe had answered each of Ben's questions without once giving the impression he was bothered by Ben's persistence. Whether Sara wanted to admit it or not, the fact that Gabe had the ability to be so patient with her son won him big points in her favor.

She chanced a glance in his direction.

He looked over at her and said, "I think Ben finally wore himself out."

Sara glanced behind her. Ben was fast asleep, both arms clutched tightly around Thunder, a touch of icing she'd missed with her napkin still clinging to his left cheek.

"Thanks for being so patient with him," Sara said. "Ben's nonstop questions can get rather annoying."

"Not to me," he said. "I'm glad he's interested in life on the ranch."

Sara didn't answer.

He glanced over at her again. "And what about you? How are you holding up?"

His question caught her completely off guard.

"I'm fine," Sara lied.

His expression said he didn't believe her but he changed the subject.

"It's a twelve-hour trip to Redstone. I thought we'd drive to just north of Albuquerque then stop for the night. That will put us halfway and break up the trip for Ben."

Again, Sara was surprised by his insight. Keeping Ben strapped in his booster seat for twelve hours would have been a real challenge.

"I called ahead and made reservations," he said. "Separate rooms, of course," he added for clarity.

"Of course," Sara was quick to answer.

The silence hung between them for a second.

Gabe turned his attention back to the highway.

Sara pretended to look out the window again.

But her thoughts kept going back to the conversation they'd had the previous evening. Gabe had assured her the only relationship he ever hoped to foster between them was a friendship. Knowing he had no personal interest in her should have been a huge relief.

But it wasn't.

Not really.

Gabe's firm declaration that he wasn't interested in her personally had dragged up old feelings. Feelings of the way she'd always felt with each new foster family. They'd taken her in, sure. And they'd provided for her adequately. But not one of her foster families had ever been truly interested in her personally.

She'd often wondered if that's why she'd been such an easy target for Billy. He had been the first person to ever seem genuinely interested in her. Of course, that, too, had been a lie. Just like the lie Billy had fed her about taking her with him when he left Houston.

She'd felt like such a fool that morning when she arrived at the rodeo grounds, suitcase in hand, only to find Billy had left without her. But not because she loved him. She hadn't known Billy long enough to fall in love.

Billy had represented a chance to free herself from her past. A chance to finally be in the company of people who truly *liked* her. Not people who were being paid by the state of Texas to tolerate her because she had a lousy mother who couldn't stay out of trouble.

Sara had let her guard down.

And she'd never seen Billy again.

But at least Gabe had been honest with her. At least she knew where she stood with him. She glanced in his direction again, wishing her stomach didn't do major flip-flops every time she looked at him. But his genuine kindness and his complete devotion to her son kept tugging on her heartstrings.

Qualities like those would win any mother's heart.

Except her heart was the last thing Gabe wanted.

He'd made it perfectly clear from the moment she met him that his only interest was in Ben. He'd offered to marry her because of Ben. He'd offered her a home because of Ben. He'd offered her a chance for new life because of Ben. Her son was the only common bond she and Gabe Coulter would ever have. She had to accept that.

Officially they were a family now—but only on paper.

"Blood kin is blood kin," he'd told her once.

And that left Sara where she'd always been.

The outsider—yet again.

CHAPTER SIX

"THOSE MOUNTAINS straight ahead are the Ragged Mountains," Gabe said the next day as they neared the end of their trip. "The Crested-C sits right in the middle of that big forest."

"Wow," Ben said in awe.

Sara agreed, but she didn't say so. The snow-capped mountains in the distance were simply breathtaking.

"The elevation reaches over ten thousand feet on some of the peaks, and the snow never melts there," Gabe said. "But the elevation at the ranch is only around seven thousand feet. The summer days are nice and mild. And the summer nights are just chilly enough to be comfortable."

"Do any bears live in those mountains, Uncle Gabe?"

"You bet they do, Ben. And there are cougars and elk, and lots of deer and beaver. We have our share of coyotes, too," Gabe added, "and that's why we keep dogs like Bess on the ranch. Old

Bess can smell a coyote a mile away. The minute she starts barking, we know to keep our eye on the livestock."

"Did you hear that, Mom? We'll have to watch out for those mean old coyotes."

Sara only nodded. But she kept thinking to herself that Ben having cougars, bears and coyotes for neighbors was far less threatening than the street gangs, drugs and violence she'd faced at his age living in the southwest slums of Houston.

"There's an eagle's nest on the cliffs above the ranch," Gabe said. "You can watch eagles fish for trout in the river right from the front porch."

"Did you hear, Mom? Real eagles," Ben said in wonder.

Sara turned her head and smiled at Ben, trying to remember when she'd seen her son so excited. She couldn't.

She'd had a long talk with herself as she lay awake the previous night, staring at the ceiling in the hotel room, her son asleep and snuggled close beside her. And she'd made a silent promise to Ben that she was going to stop feeling sorry for herself and embrace the chance to make things work.

Ben needed a strong male influence in his life, and Gabe was willing to give him that. The least she could do was make the transition into their new life as easy as possible for all of them. And with that thought in mind, Sara decided it was time to stop looking out the window and join the conversation.

She pointed to the side of the road when a head popped up out of a hole to look at them. "Look at that cute little animal, Ben."

"Ah, Mom," Ben said with typical male disgust. "That's just a silly prairie dog. You see them all the time."

When Sara glanced at Gabe, the amused look on his face told her he'd seen through her ploy. But he made no attempt to give her away.

"Maybe your mom would like to ask a few questions," Gabe said, seeming willing to include her in the conversation now that she'd shown a little interest.

"Yeah, Mom. What do you want to know?" Ben mimicked.

Sara wasn't sure what to ask now that she had full male attention. "Oh, I don't know," she finally said. "Is the house at the ranch a large house?"

"It's a two-story log house that's been added on to over the years," Gabe said, glancing over at her. "The main part of the house is the cabin my grandfather built when he first came out west and bought the property."

He paused for a moment before he said, "Let's see, there are fourteen rooms in all if you count the three bathrooms. There's a formal living room and dining room. A big kitchen. And I have an office at the house." He glanced behind him and smiled at Ben when he said, "And there's a den with a television that you can use as your playroom, Ben."

He looked back at Sara and said, "There are five bedrooms in all. I wish I could offer you the privacy of the master bedroom and bath on the first floor, Sara, but they belong to my ranch foreman. Smitty walks with a cane now and the stairs are hard for him to manage."

Sara sent him a puzzled look. "But I thought you said your ranch hands lived in a bunkhouse on the property."

"Smitty's more family than he is my ranch foreman," Gabe said. "He moved into the house and took over the cooking after my mother died. He knows more about ranching than I'll ever know. If it hadn't been for Smitty, I wouldn't have been able to hold on to the ranch."

"And this Smitty," Sara asked, "have you told him you're bringing a wife back to the ranch along with your nephew?"

He hesitated for a second. "Yes. I talked to Smitty yesterday. Why?"

"Well, you just said Smitty's been taking care of your house since your mother died," Sara said.

"It only seems logical he might not be that receptive to handing the reins over to someone else."

"Don't worry about Smitty," he said. "It might take a few weeks, but he'll get used to the idea of having you and Ben around."

Sara started to comment, but something held her back.

For the first time, it registered that she and Ben weren't the only ones whose lives were going to be changed drastically. Gabe was going to have to make more than a few adjustments in his life now that he had a wife and a child to consider. And thinking about Gabe made Sara wonder who else might have to get used to the idea that he'd decided to bring a new wife home to Redstone.

You idiot, Sara thought, scolding herself for not thinking of it before. There was no way a man like Gabe would be lacking for female attention. Gabe Coulter was every woman's fantasy, all wrapped up in a faded denim package and tied with one gigantic sex-appeal bow.

"Is there anyone else you should tell me about?" Sara asked. "Someone who might be a little upset you're bringing home a ready-made family?"

His flinch was unmistakable.

He glanced at Sara for a moment, then back at the road. "No one *I'm* concerned about," was his only answer.

Sara dropped the subject, but his ambiguous answer led her to believe there certainly was a disgruntled lady somewhere in Redstone. A lady who had to be stewing over the fact that Gabe had tossed aside his own plans in order to take responsibility for his dead brother's son.

GABE COULD HAVE bypassed Redstone and taken the back road out to the Crested-C, but he chose instead to drive through the center of his hometown. To Gabe's way of thinking, the sooner people got a good look at his new family, the sooner the gossip would die down and they could get on with starting a new life.

As much as he loved Smitty, Gabe had no doubt the old gossip had made a beeline to the country store directly after he'd called with the news. Gabe also knew Smitty would have wasted no time venting his frustration that Gabe had gone against his advice and had been foolish enough to marry the boy's mother in order to bring his nephew home.

Privacy in a small town was nonexistent. Especially in a town as small as Redstone, where the biggest news of the day was usually whether the old Dalmatian at the fire hall made it all the way down Redstone Boulevard and back. Gabe knew any attempt to conceal his new family would be treated as cowardice.

And he was no coward.

By driving through the center of town on a busy Saturday afternoon, Gabe knew he was making an unfaltering statement. He was telling everyone in Redstone that he was confident in his decision whether anyone liked it or not.

He threw his hand up for an occasional wave, and accepted the nods and greetings from the people who stopped what they were doing long enough to gawk at his two passengers. But it wasn't until they were nearing the end of town that Gabe chanced another glance at Sara.

She'd been sitting ramrod straight in her seat since he first drove into town. Her eyes were still focused straight ahead, but Gabe suspected as intuitive as she'd been about Smitty and any possible love interest in his life, the new Mrs. Coulter was more than aware why he'd purposely taken her on his little tour.

As if she'd read his mind, she suddenly looked over at him and said, "Well? Do you think we passed inspection?"

Gabe knew better than to insult her by pretending he hadn't put them on display. "Folks in Redstone are nosy, Sara, but they're also practical. We're legally married and they'll accept you and Ben without question."

Her expression said she was doubtful.

But Gabe had told her the truth.

Redstone would accept Sara.

Would Sara, however, decide to accept Redstone?

As he took the gravel road that would finally lead his new family home, Gabe suddenly realized that getting Sara to agree to come to Colorado had been the easy part.

Keeping Sara in Colorado would be the challenge.

SARA HELD her breath as they passed under two towering gate posts supporting a large sign with the Crested-C logo carved deep into the stained cedar. The setting was definitely rustic, but something about entering through the massive gate actually had a royal feel to it.

A fairy tale Sara loved as a child flashed through her mind. In the story, a handsome prince from a faraway kingdom had ridden into a modest village searching for a young maiden to become his princess bride. Though complete strangers, the maiden had eagerly accepted his proposal. They'd ridden away together on his gallant white stallion, headed for his kingdom so the new princess could give the prince the one thing he wanted most of all: an heir to his throne.

Sara suppressed a sigh.

A handsome stranger was taking her off to his

kingdom. And Ben even represented an heir to the Crested-C Ranch. Unfortunately, the white pickup truck was no gallant stallion; she was no longer a young maiden, and there would be no fairy-tale romance waiting at the end of her journey.

Her heart might have believed that if Gabe hadn't suddenly looked over at her and smiled.

"We're almost there," he said, prompting Ben to squirm in his booster seat, trying his best to see out the windshield.

Sara was doing a bit of squirming herself. They were now traveling up the mountain on a narrow gravel road that seemed to be etched out of the hillside. She squeezed her eyes shut when the truck inched dangerously close to the edge of the steep ravine.

Her eyes snapped back open when Ben squealed. "Mom! Horses!"

A magnificent herd of horses was grazing unconcernedly on plush green grass in the meadow up ahead. At the sound of the approaching truck, several of the horses shied away from the fence and bolted across the meadow, delighting Ben even more. Even Sara had to admit she'd never seen a more spectacular setting. With the snowcapped mountains above them, the entire scene looked like something from a postcard at a souvenir shop.

"The house is just ahead," Gabe told them, and seconds later Sara saw the outline of a log-and-rock structure that was large enough to double as a small hotel.

Ben gave his usual response. "Wow."

And Sara marveled. "The house is enormous."

But when she glanced over at Gabe, his brow was furrowed and a scowl had settled on his handsome face. Sara followed his gaze back to the house. Two figures were standing on the front porch. And when the truck got closer, Sara felt her own breath catch in her throat.

One of the figures was definitely female.

Sara knew without question that the curvaceous figure, standing on the porch beside a stooped older man she presumed to be Smitty, had to match Gabe's flippant definition of "no one *I'm* concerned about."

"This should be interesting," Sara said out loud.

CHAPTER SEVEN

THE LAST PERSON Gabe wanted to find on his front porch when he brought his new family home was Veronica Kincaid. But there she was. As big as life, and obviously itching for a fight.

He'd known, of course, he'd have to face Ronnie sooner or later. But Gabe had assumed it would be *later,* and on his own terms.

He stole another look at Sara and immediately regretted his decision to sidestep the issue when she'd pointedly asked him about *anyone* being unhappy with his decision. But Gabe could come closer to explaining Einstein's theory of relativity than he could to explaining his misguided relationship with Ronnie Kincaid.

For years, everyone had assumed he and Ronnie would end up together. Mainly because Ronnie's ranch, the Flying-K, bordered Gabe's own property. And next to the Crested-C, the Flying-K was the largest ranch in Pitkin County.

But Gabe knew people also took their relationship for granted because Ronnie spent most of her time telling anyone who would listen that she intended to marry him come hell or high water. The feeling, however, had never been mutual.

And not because the lady wasn't pleasing to the eye.

Ronnie was downright beautiful. They'd even had a few lust-filled moments over the years—after all, he was only human. But lust was one thing. And settling down with any woman on a permanent basis wasn't going to happen.

Especially not Ronnie.

Gabe would sooner cuddle up with a timber rattler than he would his pushy neighbor. Ronnie was cold, she was ruthless, and she was willing to bulldoze over anything or anyone in her path to get what she wanted. If she hadn't been so stubborn, Gabe suspected she would have moved on and found some other guy to badger and harass. But the more he'd ignored her, the more determined Ronnie had become to reel him in. She'd even gone as far as bragging that she'd have him at the altar by Christmas this year.

And that's why Ronnie was standing on his porch now. Her own bragging had made her a laughingstock.

And *no one* laughed at Ronnie Kincaid.

Gabe reluctantly brought the truck to a stop

several yards away, fully aware of the fury that awaited him. "If you don't mind," he told Sara, "I'd rather you and Ben wait here for a few minutes."

When Sara nodded in agreement, Gabe headed toward the two surly figures who were now glaring at him.

"IS UNCLE GABE in trouble, Mom? Those people sound really mad."

"Your uncle can take care of himself," Sara told her son, handing Ben a coloring book to distract him from the angry voices that reached them.

Ben taken care of, Sara looked back at the porch.

The woman was strikingly beautiful.

And the way Gabe took her firmly by the arm and led her around the side of the house, Sara knew this woman had a past with Gabe—an intimate past. One he'd tossed aside for Ben. It was all Sara could do to keep from opening the door and throwing up out of pure guilt.

She'd been so busy feeling sorry for herself she hadn't stopped to realize the person making the ultimate sacrifice wasn't her at all—it was Gabe. It was Gabe's world they were intruding upon. Gabe's plans they were ruining. Gabe's life they were changing.

The old man was still glued to the spot on the porch, leaning on a cane and holding a suitcase in his free hand. When he frowned in Sara's direction, another wave of guilt swept over her.

"Stay in the truck, Ben," Sara ordered.

She made her way steadily to where the old man was standing. And when she reached the bottom step, Sara shielded her eyes from the sun with her hand and met the man's angry regard.

"I'm Sara," she offered, "and you must be Smitty."

"That's what my *friends* call me." The old man grunted, dismissing her coldly.

Sara refused to be put off by his rudeness.

"I couldn't help but overhear that you're leaving," Sara told him. "If you're leaving because of me and my son, I'm truly sorry."

He glanced in her direction briefly, but remained unyielding. "Ain't it a little late to be sorry? You got what you wanted. Gabe married you."

Sara dropped her hand and pretended to stare out over the ranch the same way Smitty was pretending to do. "Yes, Gabe and I did get married," Sara said. "And we've agreed if things aren't working after six months, Ben and I will leave. But I'll leave right now before I run you out of your own home. And I mean that sincerely."

Smitty still refused to look at her. "Don't you worry about me, missy," he said. "I've made my own arrangements. Ronnie Kincaid's been trying to steal me away from Gabe for years. She's here to pick me up now. I'm her new foreman over at the Flying-K."

The fact that the woman was a rancher, too, had little to do with the situation, and Sara knew it. Sara hadn't missed her "How could you do this to me?" screech at Gabe. If anything, Sara suspected the woman's attempt to hire Smitty had been nothing more than a ruse to put her on the scene when Gabe drove up with his new family in tow.

Sara said, "Then I guess there's been a big misunderstanding."

He glanced in her direction, but Sara knew he was too proud to ask what she meant.

"I was under the impression Gabe really needed you on the ranch. He told me you knew more about ranching than he would ever know."

The old man stood a little straighter and actually puffed his chest out a bit. "Gabe said that, did he?"

Sara nodded innocently. "He also said you were the backbone of this ranch, and that he was glad I could take over the house and the cooking so you could get back to running the ranch the way it should be run."

She was stretching the truth, but her words seemed to be working. Smitty lowered his suitcase slowly, then shifted his weight back to his cane. "Well, I guess I could stay on at least a week or two," he grumbled, meeting her eyes fully for the first time. "Just until you get settled in, that is," he added. "Gabe can't do everything around here. He'll need someone to show you what needs to be done in the house."

"I'd really appreciate that," Sara said, but she noticed his gaze had suddenly drifted past her. When Sara turned, Ben was standing only a few feet away, accepting lavish kisses from a large black-and-white dog.

"Could you show me how to rope one of those horses so I could ride him, mister?" Ben asked, petting the dog's head with one hand while pointing to the pasture at the side of the house with the other.

When Sara glanced back at Smitty, the old man's face crumpled right before her eyes. By the time Ben and the big dog bounded up the steps, Smitty was wiping his eyes with a red and white bandanna he'd pulled from the back pocket of his overalls. He didn't object when Ben reached out and took his hand.

"Gabe said Ben looks exactly like Billy did when he was that age," Sara mentioned.

"Spittin' image," Smitty managed to say in a slightly choked voice. "And that's a fact."

"Well, can you, mister?" Ben asked, oblivious to the emotion he had stirred. "Can you get me one of those horses to ride? Uncle Gabe said I can't go near the horses unless a grown-up goes with me."

"You can call me Smitty, son," the old man said, then started down the steps with Ben leading the way. "But the first thing any good horseman learns is that you have to make friends with a horse before you can ride him."

"Will you show me how?"

"Making friends with a horse takes time," Smitty said with authority. "Now take that big roan stallion over there by the side of the fence," he said, pointing to the horse with his cane. "Old Bruiser can be real friendly, or he can be real mean. You see, it's all in the way you handle a horse, Ben...."

Sara couldn't suppress a smile as she watched the twosome stroll off in the direction of the pasture with the big dog following closely at their heels. But her smile evaporated when movement from the corner of her eye warned Sara she was no longer alone. Turning around, Sara found herself face-to-face with the woman Smitty had identified as Ronnie Kincaid.

Her jet-black hair was cut short like a man's, but it suited her. And her skin was as smooth and tanned as the expensive leather boots she wore. She was tall and she was lean. Her tight-fitting jeans showed off every inch of her long, perfect legs.

Sara immediately felt drab in this woman's presence.

She gave Sara a quick look up and down and dismissed her just as rapidly. But when she saw Smitty holding Ben up on the fence so he could rub a big chestnut horse between the ears, she stomped off in a huff toward a black Suburban that was parked at the far end of the porch. Within seconds, Sara found herself fanning away the dust left in the wake of the irate Miss Kincaid.

"Sorry about the interruption," Gabe said nonchalantly as he walked up beside her. He smiled when he looked toward the pasture. "Looks like Smitty's decided to stay on. What did you say to make him stay?"

Determined to act every bit as nonchalant as Gabe, Sara shrugged. "I told Smitty the truth. That Ben and I would leave before we ran him out of his own home."

Gabe frowned. "You aren't having second thoughts are you, Sara?"

Shouldn't I be having second thoughts after the scene I witnessed? Sara wanted to scream. His girlfriend had thrown a full-blown hissy fit right in the middle of the yard. And Gabe had the nerve to stroll up acting like the welcome committee had paid them all a social call.

But Sara took a deep breath and said, "It's

obvious us being here is causing you major problems, Gabe. We can still call this whole thing off, you know. Whether you believe it or not, you don't owe Ben a thing."

His frown deepened at her last comment.

He pointed to the pasture where Ben and Smitty now had several horses vying for their attention. "I want you to look out there right now and tell me you can't already see that Ben belongs here."

Sara refused to admit any such thing.

"I can take care of my own problems, Sara. All you have to do is take care of Ben."

Then he was gone.

Leaving Sara standing in the yard, still shivering from Ronnie Kincaid's icy glare, and trying to convince herself she wouldn't care if the man she'd married ended up in another woman's bed when the sun went down.

GABE COULD FEEL the weight of Sara's stare as he walked toward the pasture, but he never looked back. She hadn't questioned him about the scene with Ronnie, but Gabe felt guilty for not trying to explain. At the moment, however, Gabe's belly was full of trying to talk logically to *any* member of the opposite sex.

He'd let Ronnie vent her anger, reminding her that he'd never led her on as she accused, and that she'd always known nothing serious was ever going to develop between them. He'd also pointed out that she knew full well the two of them had never discussed a wedding date—ever—and certainly not for December. And he'd told her that despite what she thought of his decision to marry his nephew's mother, the case was closed and his decision was final.

He'd managed to keep his composure through her screams and insults. He'd even taken the hard slap in the face she'd given him when they first rounded the corner of the house. It wasn't until Ronnie threatened Ben and Sara that Gabe lost control.

He'd ordered Ronnie off his property.

And in doing so, Gabe knew he'd made a bitter enemy.

Anyone would testify that Ronnie Kincaid was not someone you wanted for an enemy. And Gabe knew he'd have his hands full over the next few months trying to run interference and protect Ben and Sara from the woman's unfounded wrath.

When he reached the pasture, Gabe propped himself casually against a fence post directly beside Smitty. "Looks like your new boss left without you, old man," Gabe said. "If you need transportation over to the Flying-K, you can take the flatbed and I'll send one of the hands after it later."

Smitty adjusted his grip on Ben, who was now

leaning over the fence to pet a colt. "Oh, you'd like that, wouldn't you?" Smitty snapped. "It would be just like you to spread it all over town that I walked off the Crested-C after forty years without giving notice."

Gabe shrugged, perfectly comfortable with the bantering that had always gone on between them. "Well, it would be pretty low-down of a foreman to walk off the job without giving any notice."

"If you think you're gonna ruin *my* reputation, sonny boy, then you're badly mistaken," Smitty said.

"You're staying on, then?" Gabe egged things on a little further.

Smitty reached out to shove Bruiser's nose away when the big horse pushed his muzzle a little too close to Ben for Smitty's liking. "I'll stay a while," Smitty said. "That gal you brought home will have to be shown what needs to be done around here."

"And what about me?" Ben suddenly chimed in, reminding them that two little ears had been listening to their conversation. "You'll stay long enough to show me how to make friends with these horses, won't you, Smitty?"

"Making friends with horses takes a long time, Ben," Gabe said, sending Ben a wink.

"Not with this kid," Smitty said, patting his new

apprentice affectionately on the back. "Ben's a real natural with horses."

Gabe swallowed, hard. "Just like his grandfather."

"Just like his *uncle* and his grandfather," Smitty corrected, always determined to have the last word.

CHAPTER EIGHT

BY THE TIME Ronnie made it back to the Flying-K, she was still so angry she felt like smashing something. And it should have been Gabe's stupid face with her fist instead of slapping him openhandedly like a girl.

The bastard!

He'd been a stubborn ass forever. But Gabe's first obligation had always been to his ranch and his horses. And that's what had Ronnie so confused. The logical thing would have been to marry her and merge their two ranches.

What had Gabe done instead?

He'd married some piece of fluff from Texas who would have burst into tears had Ronnie bothered to say *boo* to the silly bitch. And all because of a dumb promise he'd made to Billy.

The stupid fool!

Storming into the house, Ronnie headed straight for the den. The fact that her father was sitting in his usual place at a card table playing solitaire didn't prevent her from walking directly to the wet bar on the far side of the room. Pouring two fingers' worth of bourbon into a tumbler, Ronnie belted it down in one easy gulp. But as she wiped her mouth with the back of her hand, she sent a hostile glare in her father's direction.

"What are you looking at?"

Ross Kincaid looked back down at the cards on the table and waited a few seconds before he said, "Isn't it a little early in the day for whiskey?"

"Mind your own damn business, Ross."

She poured herself another drink.

"Then I guess the rumor's true," he said. "Gabe really did marry the boy's mother."

Ronnie didn't answer. She took the tumbler with her and flopped onto the heavy leather sofa facing the stone fireplace. She was pissed. And the last thing she wanted was *any* advice from her father. Ross was weak and gutless. Always had been.

How else would you describe a man falling to pieces when a worthless woman like her mother walked out on them? Pathetic, that's what Ross was. Ronnie couldn't even remember her mother, but she'd had enough sense to say good riddance to her a long time ago.

But not Ross.

After her mother left he'd lost interest in everything. His life. His ranch. And most of all, his only child.

To hell with both of them, Ronnie vowed as she brought the tumbler to her lips again. She'd never needed a mother or a father. By age twelve she could ride a horse as well as any man on the ranch. By sixteen she was breaking the most difficult horses herself. And by twenty-one she was doing the bookkeeping and making all of the major decisions where the ranch was concerned.

And what had her stupid father been doing during that time? He'd sat uselessly in the den playing solitaire, still pining away for a woman he hadn't even seen in thirty long years.

Ronnie was the reason they still had a roof over their heads. *She* was responsible for making the Flying-K one of the most successful horse ranches in the state of Colorado. So *any* advice from dear Papa was not damned welcomed.

"I did you a huge disservice by not letting your mother take you with her when she left," Ross said, as if he'd known exactly what Ronnie had been thinking.

"Like hell, you did." Ronnie snorted. To annoy him, she drained every drop of the whiskey in her tumbler.

He pretended not to notice, his eyes still focused on the cards he was holding. And just when Ronnie thought she'd been successful at putting an end to any phony father-daughter chat, Ross said, "I've stood by and watched this ranch become your whole life. And I made a grave mistake in doing that. Maybe if you'd gone with your mother, maybe then—"

"What?" Ronnie shouted. "Maybe I would have followed in dear old Mommy's footsteps? Spent my time jet-setting from here to there, dining on Russian caviar and drinking champagne instead of working my ass off to keep us from losing this ranch?"

"Maybe you wouldn't have turned out so—" he rubbed a hand over his forehead "—callous."

"*Callous?* I'll tell you what's callous, Ross. Callous is being more worried about finding a new wrinkle in the mirror than the fact you have a daughter you haven't seen since she was two years old. So don't you dare call me callous. Save callous for the woman who walked out on both of us."

She'd gotten herself so worked up she jumped up from the sofa and smashed her empty tumbler against the rock hearth of the fireplace. Turning to face her father, Ronnie said, "This ranch will always be my life. And whether you'll ever admit it or not, I do a damn fine job running it."

Ross shuffled his cards, still never looking in her direction. "Then why don't you do that,

Veronica? Why don't you concentrate on running *this* ranch and leave Gabe Coulter alone? If I thought you actually loved the man, it might be different. But we both know all you've ever wanted is Gabe's land."

Ronnie didn't deny it.

Instead she mocked her father's words. "What did love ever get you, Ross? I'll tell you what love got you. Nothing. Except a lifetime of living in the past."

He looked directly at her for the first time. "We're not talking about me. We're talking about you. And I know my own daughter. You don't like to lose. But leave Gabe alone. He's a good man."

Ronnie threw her head back and laughed. "I'll never leave Gabe alone. We're two of a kind, me and Gabe. We're ranchers first. And everything else comes second."

"Not anymore, Ronnie. Gabe has a family now."

"We had a family, too, but that didn't keep my mother here, did it?"

His flinch made Ronnie smile.

She walked around the sofa and leaned over her father, her hands braced on the card table in front of him. "That little twit Gabe brought home won't last a week. And when she skips town the same way my sorry mother did, I'll be right here where I've always been. Waiting for Gabe to come to his senses so we can merge the Flying-K and the Crested-C and have the largest damn horse ranch in the state of Colorado."

She headed for the door, but paused before walking out.

"You are right about one thing though, Ross. I don't like to lose. And I intend to do everything in my power to make sure Miss Texas leaves Redstone as fast as her pretty little ass breezed into town."

Her say over, Ronnie stormed out of the house and headed for the barn, the new scowl on her face put there by another old man who had taken Gabe's side that day. She should have known that fool Smitty would back down the minute Gabe got home. Now she'd have to do some major damage control. She'd have to swallow her pride and formally ask her ranch foreman to stay.

Not that she was really worried about Charlie Biggs leaving. Hell, you couldn't blow Charlie off the Flying-K with a stick of dynamite. She hadn't missed the way Charlie looked at her. She could feel his eyes undressing her with every move she made.

And now that Gabe had gone and got himself married?

No, Charlie wouldn't be in any big hurry to leave.

He'd hang around for sure now, thinking he might get lucky. Which wasn't a bad idea when Ronnie thought about it.

She'd be damned if she let the whole town laugh at her behind her back. She'd show them. All of them. And she'd start by letting word get around town that she'd been too busy screwing Charlie's brains out to even care that Gabe Coulter got married.

Stepping inside the open barn door, Ronnie looked around first, relieved to see no one else was present except the man she'd come to see. Eating crow had never been her strong point and she damn sure didn't want an audience when she did it.

Her focus settled on Charlie.

He was stripped down, wearing nothing but his jeans, his bare back to her as he rubbed down a saddle he had on the workbench before him. Her gaze swept across his broad muscled shoulders, then downward, settling on one fine cowboy ass if she had to say so herself. Had Charlie been a rancher instead of a ranch hand, she would have chosen him over Gabe Coulter any day of the week.

Charlie was a handsome devil. Hair black as a raven's wing—gray eyes like a wolf.

And flirting with the devil was exactly what she needed after Gabe made her out to be a first-class fool. Ronnie took a step in Charlie's direction. And finally sensing her presence, he glanced over his shoulder at her.

It was now or never to make amends.

"You're staying on as foreman," Ronnie told rather than asked him.

"Not interested," he said, and went back to work on the saddle.

Ronnie rolled her eyes.

She really hadn't expected any less. They'd had a huge fight earlier that morning when she'd told Charlie she was bringing Smitty in as acting foreman. Charlie had seen right through her intentions. Now he was going to make her beg.

But she'd do her begging her own way.

Ronnie walked over and casually propped herself against the workbench facing Charlie. With her elbows resting on the surface, all it took was a slight forward thrust of her breasts. And, presto! The front of her shirt popped open enough to give Charlie a peek at anything he wanted to see.

His gaze immediately went to her cleavage.

"Don't be an ass, Charlie. You know I pay you more than anyone else pays a foreman around here."

He looked away. "Maybe I'm not staying around here. Maybe it's time I moved on."

He went back to work on the saddle.

Hard muscles rippled.

Healthy biceps flexed.

Ronnie inched a little closer to him.

"But surely we can think of something that might entice you to stay," Ronnie said, running the tip of her finger seductively up the full length of Charlie's bare arm.

She felt him tense under her touch.

He put down the saddle soap and looked at her. "Yeah," he said, "I can think of one thing that might make me stay."

Ronnie smiled.

"I want to hear you say you're through making an idiot of yourself over Gabe Coulter."

Her hand shot forward to slap him.

Charlie caught her arm midair.

Ronnie could see the lust in his eyes. And Lord, how it did turn her on. Just once, she'd love to know what it felt like to be taken by a man who truly wanted her—not just because she'd made herself convenient.

Too bad about her pride, though. "Get off my property. Now!"

"I'll get off your property," Charlie said. "But not until I show you what you'll be missing when I'm gone."

Ronnie gasped when he jerked her forward. She tried to fight back, but he dragged her with him into the tack room. And when he kicked the door shut behind them, he pushed her roughly up against the plank wall and pinned her hands above her head with one strong arm.

Their gazes locked in a fiery battle of wills.

Ronnie, daring him to touch her.

Charlie, daring her to stop him.

His free hand roamed down her neck. Slowly, he unbuttoned the front of her shirt. Ronnie held her breath as his hand slid inside her bra. And when he gave her nipple a hard but ever-so-pleasurable squeeze, Ronnie moaned in spite of herself.

Instantly, his hot mouth came down on hers. Ronnie kissed him back as forcefully.

She was much too aroused to push Charlie away, and way too turned-on to care. His hand slid from her breast, down her stomach, fumbling for the zipper of her jeans. She gasped again when his fingers slid boldly between her legs. And though she bit down hard on her lower lip trying to resist him, the shiver of sheer pleasure running through her body left her crying for more.

For the first time in her life, Ronnie surrendered.

And Charlie took complete control.

CHAPTER NINE

BY THE END of her third week on the ranch, every muscle in Sara's body ached from the exertion of removing fifteen years of dirt and grime from the house she and her son now called home. Gabe had warned her Smitty ran off every cleaning lady he'd tried to hire over the years, but nothing could have prepared Sara for an all-male perspective of the acceptable level of *clean.*

Sara had washed everything from curtains to bed linens. She'd chased cobwebs and dust bunnies until they often showed up in her dreams as full-blown monsters.

She'd never been immune to hard work. But Sara soon found that taking on the responsibility of running a house, being a full-time mom to an active five-year-old and cooking three meals a day for a bunch of hungry ranch hands who wolfed down every morsel she placed in front of them was a never-ending task. More than once it crossed her mind that any woman who had the audacity to label being a housewife *mindless* work, did so only in fear that someone might ask her to take on such an overpowering assignment.

For Sara, there were no scheduled coffee breaks, no relaxing lunch hours, nor did she have any coworkers to help with the multitude of duties she performed on a daily basis. In a nutshell, she was it. And the enormous amount of organizational skills required to keep a mental note of what her son was doing, tend to a meal in the oven, supervise the laundry and dust and vacuum a fourteen-room house, was extremely overwhelming.

There were days when Sara would run from one task to another at such a maddening speed, she contemplated having Smitty shop for a pair of roller blades when he made his daily trip into Redstone. Thankfully, Smitty *did* make those daily trips into town for their supplies. Had shopping also been added to her vast list of duties, Sara would have collected her son and headed back to Texas after her second day on the ranch.

Life at the Crested-C began at sunrise and it ended shortly after dusk. And though a lesser woman would have admitted defeat, Sara had never been happier.

For the first time in her life, she had the joy of experiencing what it was like to be part of a real family. Granted, it wasn't a typical family, but it was a family nonetheless. And nothing pleased Sara more than sitting at the opposite end of the large dining room table from Gabe, watching while seven burly cowboys folded their hands politely and waited for Ben to deliver his short "God is Great" prayer of thanks.

Sara never wanted to be anywhere else.

Especially since their new lifestyle was having such a positive effect on her son. Ben had adapted to their new surroundings so quickly it scared Sara. Not only had he abandoned his mother's side to become Smitty's constant shadow, but her five-year-old baby had jumped at the chance to have his own bedroom. Ironically, that happened to be Billy's old bedroom—still adorned with life-size posters of the acclaimed rodeo star, and lined with the multiple ribbons and trophies Billy had won over the years.

At first, it had bothered Sara to be in a room where Billy's presence was everywhere. But she eventually found comfort reading to Ben every night with Billy smiling down at them. It was almost as if Billy were trying to tell her he was sorry. And that he couldn't have been more pleased to have his son home.

Being surrounded by his father's possessions seemed to have given Ben a sense of comfort, too. And for that, Sara would be eternally grateful.

Unlike her own unanswered questions about a father she never knew, for Ben, there would be no unanswered questions. Billy had become real for Ben. And as long as Gabe and Smitty were around, Sara knew her son would have answers for anything he ever wanted to know about his father.

The hardest part of Sara's new life were those moments she spent in her own bedroom at night before she gave in to the exhaustion of the day and let sleep mercifully claim her. It was then that her old doubts and fears crept in to make her leery of her new peace and happiness.

Do you really think this can last? Didn't you give Gabe the perfect out by agreeing to have the marriage annulled in six months if the arrangement wasn't working?

And that had become Sara's latest fear.

What if things didn't work out? What was she going to tell Ben then? Even thinking about how devastated her son would be if they had to leave the ranch terrified Sara.

And that's why many nights found her tossing and turning when such disturbing questions refused to leave her alone. Especially when the questions took on an even deeper level of cruelty.

Where do you think Gabe runs off to every night? her troubled thoughts would nag her. *Do you really think he'll stay in a phony marriage when he has a woman like Ronnie Kincaid waiting in the wings? You're just his housekeeper, remember? The woman he puts up with because you happen to be his nephew's mother.*

Those were the thoughts that hurt the deepest, constantly reminding Sara exactly where she fit into the whole scheme of things. She would never be anything more to Gabe than his nephew's mother. And the fragile bond that was slowly forming between them would never be anything more than the friendship Gabe said he wanted based solely on the mutual concern they shared for her son.

Of course, Sara told herself she was willing to settle for nothing but friendship from Gabe. That her life at the ranch would be complete, as long as she had the opportunity to watch her son grow into a good and honest man.

A man who would take his commitments seriously.

A man who would be kind and giving.

A man who was admired and respected by his peers.

A man like Gabe.

The same man who was winning tiny pieces of Sara's watchful heart with each passing day.

THE FULL MOON BATHED the house in a silvery light when Gabe turned off his headlights and let the truck coast into the circular driveway. The long drives he'd been taking over the past three weeks were beginning to get the better of him. Still, driving around aimlessly and trying to clear his head was better than lying wide awake wondering what type of silky nightgown the woman in the room next to his was wearing while she slept.

At first, he'd hoped the card game in the bunkhouse would be the perfect diversion for the growing physical attraction he was feeling for Sara. But he'd taken such a hard ribbing from his ranch hands about the *strip poker* they'd be playing if they had a pretty new wife like Sara, he'd given up on that idea.

Not that he could really blame his rowdy hands for thinking he was fifty kinds of crazy. Hell, all of them were already half in love with Sara. Even Smitty liked her, though he'd yet to admit it.

And that's what had Gabe so confused.

He'd expected to have a mutiny on his hands. Not a bunch of lovesick cowpokes.

Yet, when Gabe thought about it, who could really blame the guys for being smitten with Sara? She had a pinup-model figure, sure. But it was more than that.

Maybe the dresses she wore were part of it. She always looked so feminine: her dark hair swept up on top of her head, a few stray tendrils caressing her neck; an apron tied around her tiny waist; the long skirts of her dresses only allowing a peek at an ankle now and then.

She was sexy as hell.

But she was also as wholesome as motherhood, apple pie and "The Star-Spangled Banner" all rolled into one. And what cowboy had ever been able to resist a combination like that one?

None Gabe knew of.

He'd also been amazed by the way she'd taken over the household with such ease. Everything from one end of the house to the other had been spit-shined and polished to the point that he, Smitty and the rest of the hands were checking to make sure their boots were clean before they entered the house.

And who would have ever expected that to happen?

Not to mention the fact Sara was a pure genius in the kitchen. The meals she placed before them were so delectable the general conversation around the ranch had changed from what needed to be done on the 15,000 acres they were trying to maintain, to what Sara might be serving for supper that evening.

But the thing that impressed Gabe about Sara most was the tenderness she openly exhibited toward her son. Watching Sara lovingly smooth

Ben's hair back from his forehead for a kiss, and seeing her cuddle Ben in her lap for a hug, brought back childhood memories of Gabe's own mother. Thinking of his mother made Gabe realize that for the first time in fifteen long years he had clean clothes in his closet, fresh linens on his bed and a full stomach when the sun went down.

Gabe didn't know what more a man could want.

Or did he?

He left the truck, cursing himself for allowing Sara to invade his thoughts even one second longer. He was losing his edge. Letting his mind wander where it shouldn't. Acting like some giddy teenager experiencing his first stupid crush.

He was smarter than that.

Stronger than that.

He had a ranch to run, dammit.

With that thought in mind Gabe headed for the back porch and entered through the kitchen where the rear stairs would take him to the second floor and his own bedroom. To his relief, other than the ticking of his mother's old grandfather clock, the house was quiet.

He reached his bedroom door without interruption. A sudden urge sent him down the hallway to check on his nephew—the same way he'd always checked in on Billy before he turned in himself.

The bedroom door next to his was slightly ajar. Gabe paused.

The room was dark, leading him to believe Sara was already asleep. But when he reached out to gently pull the door shut, moonlight streaming through the bedroom window allowed Gabe a quick glimpse inside the room.

The second he saw her, time jerked to a stop.

She was standing in the middle of the room with her back to the door, silently going through one of her yoga routines he'd overheard her tell Smitty helped her relax after a long, tiring day. Moonlight captured her poised silhouette, giving Gabe a mouthwatering view of her exquisite body through the thin material of the nightgown she wore.

But it was her hair that affected Gabe most.

Finally, he had his answer.

Her hair tumbled down her back in a wave of silky sable, past her waist, stopping just below her hips. He watched for almost a full minute, unable to tear his eyes away from her graceful movements until visions of her naked body hovering over his, that long hair brushing across his face, stirred more than Gabe's interest.

Ashamed for spying, Gabe stepped back from the door.

Anger quickly replaced his guilt.

How Sara had the ability to turn him completely

inside out was something he couldn't explain. He'd expected to have more self-control. But all reason went right out the window every time he looked at her. Especially when she sent him one of those damn wide-eyed looks.

Hell, maybe that's it!

Gabe frowned as he walked down the hallway.

It's her wide-eyed innocence that makes me so crazy.

And Sara had been completely innocent.

Not once in the three weeks since she'd been under his roof had she treated him with anything but the same respect he'd tried to show her. And never once had she given him the slightest indication that she could be even remotely attracted to a man like him.

Forget her! Gabe told himself and opened Ben's door. The tiny form snuggled beneath the covers caused old memories to surface. He'd only been seven years older than his brother, but he'd always felt this same protective feeling toward Billy.

Gabe listened long enough to hear the sound of Ben's even breathing before he eased the door shut. He had just started down the hallway when Sara appeared.

"Gabe?" she whispered.

Gabe's mouth went dry.

Again, moonlight from her open bedroom door

played havoc with his emotions. Bathed in the silvery light, her creamy shoulders were bare except for the thin straps of her nightgown. And though she crossed her arms in an attempt to cover herself, her actions only made Gabe more aware of the tantalizing cleavage she couldn't quite hide.

"I was just checking on Ben," Gabe whispered.

"Thanks for doing that," she said as he approached. "I left my door open so I could hear Ben if he needed me."

She didn't move until he was almost close enough to touch her. And he might have done just that had she not stepped inside the safety of her bedroom at the precise second he reached her bedroom door.

"Sleep well," she said as she shut her door.

Yeah, right! There wasn't a chance in hell he'd sleep at all now.

And that's why he had to stop running from the situation and face it head-on. No more late-night drives. No more doubting his ability to handle the situation.

He could do this.

It was time to cowboy up and deal.

Just like he'd always done.

CHAPTER TEN

SARA PUT AWAY the last of Ben's toys in the den, turned out the light and headed toward the front staircase. She paused when she saw the light coming from Gabe's office. He'd surprised her all week by staying home every night, making Sara suspect a lover's spat.

Pressure from Ronnie, no doubt. Insisting Gabe put an end to his phony marriage.

And after her first full month on the ranch, even Sara was beginning to think putting an end to their marriage might be the wise thing to do. At least where she and Gabe were concerned.

Oh, they'd managed to tiptoe around each other. They'd been overly polite. They'd even managed to pretend they weren't two healthy adults in a most uncomfortable situation.

But they *were* two healthy adults.

And Sara hadn't missed the desire she'd seen in his eyes the night they'd run into each other in the hallway when Gabe was checking on Ben.

Run while you still can, her gut instinct told her.

Sara would have done that, if, like always, Ben wasn't her main concern. But in one short month, she'd watched her five-year-old transform into a little-boy version of the other men on the ranch, complete with a closet full of western clothing Smitty had brought home shortly after their arrival.

"Now don't throw a fit," Smitty had told her rather condescendingly when he handed Ben the packages. "The boy needs proper clothing if he's gonna tag around the ranch after me. Them shorty pants you put on him ain't gonna protect his legs while he's learning to ride. And them tennis shoes sure won't protect Ben's feet if he gets too close to a horse's hoof."

Ben had been so delighted with his new clothes—his cowboy hat and his boots—Sara hadn't seen the point in arguing. Especially when Smitty educated her further by pointing out that tailored western-style shirts wouldn't hang up on fence posts like Ben's assortment of loose-fitting T-shirts, and that the string on Ben's new cowboy hat was there for a reason.

"Ain't got time to chase that baseball cap of Ben's all over the corral," Smitty had said with a snort. "The boy needs a good hat that'll stay on his head and keep the sun out of his eyes."

Of course, the clothing had been one of the

many concessions Sara found herself making where Ben was concerned. Although Gabe had asked her permission first, Ben now had his very own pony. Ben had promptly named the pony Lightning to go along with his toy horse Thunder.

And since last week, Sara had pretended she wasn't aware that Smitty was helping Ben sneak one of Bess's pups up to Ben's room every night after she delivered her final good-night kiss. Even Bandit seemed to be in on the conspiracy. Not once had Sara heard the slightest whimper out of the small fur ball. Even when she went into Ben's bedroom during the night to adjust his covers, the only telltale sign that the pup was in the room was a tiny black nose that sometimes poked out from beneath Ben's bed.

So no, running like hell wasn't an option.

At least not yet.

Sara took a deep breath and turned toward the stairs. She was already rehearsing the casual good-night she planned to offer when she passed Gabe's office doorway. She had the word on the tip of her tongue when Gabe called out her name.

"Got a minute?"

Forcing a smile, Sara entered his office. She took a seat when Gabe motioned to the chair in front of his desk.

He slid an envelope across his desk in her direction and smiled. "I only do payroll once a month," he said. "The check inside belongs to you. The ten-dollar bill is Ben's allowance. I made the mistake of telling Ben I got a monthly allowance when I was a kid. He hasn't let me forget that."

Sara stared at the envelope, but she made no attempt to pick it up.

"I'm not sure I understand," Sara told him. "About the check, I mean. Not about Ben's allowance."

"Family tradition," Gabe told her. "My mother was of the opinion that she worked as hard as any man on the ranch and she expected a paycheck once a month like everyone else. You've done a remarkable job making this place livable again, Sara. If anyone deserves a paycheck for what they do around here, it's you."

"Thank you."

She picked up the envelope, but she didn't open it. She stuffed it into the front pocket of her dress, amazed once again over Gabe's generosity. The week after they arrived, he'd purchased a new Jeep Cherokee and had given her the keys as her own means of transportation. She'd only driven it once into town—the result of another generous offer from Gabe. He'd called ahead and arranged for his personal banker to assist her in setting up her own bank account so she could deposit the money she'd been able to save in Conrad into an interest-bearing account. He'd also handed her a credit card when she'd pointed out that many of the draperies and most of the towels and the bedding in the house needed to he replaced. She'd made those purchases online on Gabe's computer, since the nearest shopping mall was over one hundred miles away in Grand Junction.

Offering her access to his computer had also allowed her to e-mail Annie and Dessie at least once a week to keep in touch. She was always careful to keep that correspondence focused strictly on Ben and how well he was doing on the ranch. Not that she thought Gabe would stoop so low as to read her e-mail. But as life had often taught her, it never hurt to stay on the safe side.

At every turn, Gabe had gone out of his way to provide her with everything she and Ben needed to transition smoothly into their new lives on the ranch. So why did she still feel so uncomfortable in this man's presence?

Sara glanced in his direction again.

He was settled comfortably back in his chair with a booted foot propped casually on one knee. And that's when Sara realized her heart knew the answer about why she was always so nervous in Gabe's presence whether she was willing to admit it or not.

Gabe totally captivated her.

Just looking at him now made Sara's pulse

quicken and her heart pound. And when his blue eyes suddenly met hers, the intense look he gave her affected Sara as deeply as a sensuous caress against her bare flesh.

"How do you think Ben's doing?" he asked, snapping Sara's thoughts back to the conversation. "Do you think he's adjusting to the ranch okay?"

Sara laughed. "The way you and Smitty spoil the child? How could Ben not like it here?"

He laughed along with her. "Ben's quite a kid," he said, his expression displaying the obvious affection he felt for her son. "And what about you? How are you adjusting to life here?"

Sara blinked at his question.

She and Gabe had daily discussions about everything from Ben's activities to household purchases and problems, but he always caught her off guard when he pointedly asked about her. She started to tell him she'd never been happier. Until the thought crossed her mind that might not be the answer Gabe wanted. That, instead, maybe he was hoping she would say ranch life didn't suit her at all—that she was even considering leaving Ben at the ranch and starting a new life on her own.

After all, wasn't that what Gabe said he wanted that day at the jail? For her to take Billy's insurance money and start a new life, but to leave Ben with him?

"Is there a problem?" Sara asked, automatically taking the defensive.

He looked at her funny. "No," he said, "there isn't a problem at all. As far as I'm concerned, things couldn't be working out any better. I was just worried you might be bored stuck out here in the middle of nowhere."

"I have an active five-year-old, and more than enough to keep me busy around here, Gabe. I don't have time to be bored."

He nodded, absently tapping his pencil against his desk blotter. "I realize that, Sara, but you aren't a slave to this ranch seven days a week. Feel free to take time off for yourself whenever you want."

"Thanks, I will," Sara said.

He kept impaling her with long, searching looks.

Sara stood, eager to end their meeting. Being in the room alone with him already had her mind wandering into dangerous territory. But he seemed to have something else on his mind. And as those blue eyes covered her face again, Sara wondered if her growing feelings for him were so transparent Gabe might be picking up on the fact that it was all she could do to keep from taking him by the hand and leading him upstairs to her bedroom to fulfill the fantasies she had about him when she was alone.

She needed to get out of there. Now.

"Well, if there isn't anything else, I think I'll go to bed," Sara said, practically sprinting for the door.

"There is one more thing."

Bracing herself, Sara turned.

"Saturday is the Fourth of July," he said, "and Smitty and the boys and I are always invited over to celebrate with our nearest neighbors Joe and Betsy Graham."

"And you want Ben to go with you?" Sara asked, assuming that was the next question.

"Actually," he said, "I was thinking about giving Betsy a break from being hostess this year and inviting the Grahams over here."

"Here?" Sara echoed.

"I wanted to ask you first, of course," he added quickly. "I realize there will be extra cooking involved on your part if we celebrate here. But you can count on Betsy to bring over enough food to feed an army."

Sara chewed nervously at her bottom lip. Could she handle this? Taking care of the ranch hands was one thing, but neighbors? That was something very different.

She finally said, "The Grahams are your friends and this is your house, Gabe. You don't need my permission to invite them over whenever you want."

His expression turned serious. "I realize that,

Sara. But I was hoping this was beginning to feel like your home, too, not someplace you're just passing through."

Sara flinched at his comment.

She'd spent a lifetime *just passing through.* She wanted to believe things were going to be different in Redstone. That she and Ben could put down roots. And that Gabe's friends would accept them, as he claimed.

But what she didn't want was to explain any of that to Gabe. At least, not yet. They'd only survived one month living together as a family. It was much too soon to let down her guard.

He could still change his mind and ask them to leave.

And so, Sara said, "I'll start making arrangements tomorrow and put together a menu for Saturday."

She was trying not to sound as nervous as she felt about meeting Gabe's friends. But a dozen questions were already running through Sara's mind. How much did the Grahams know? Did they realize the marriage was in name only? Or were they expecting to find happy newlyweds waiting to greet them?

It was on the tip of Sara's tongue to ask.

But Gabe saved her the trouble when he said, "You don't have to worry about meeting Joe and Betsy, Sara. They're good people and they have a son Ben's age. Junior will be in Ben's kindergarten class. I think it will be good for Ben if he meets a friend before school starts."

Good for Ben.

Three little words.

But those three words put Sara firmly in her place.

Of course, the Grahams knew why he'd married her. The whole town of Redstone knew why he'd married her. Ben was Gabe's only concern—and always would be. The sooner she accepted that fact, the better off she'd be.

Sara wasted no time saying good-night. But she did wait until she'd closed her bedroom door before she took the envelope out of her pocket. When she saw the amount written on the check, her usual self-doubts surfaced to worry her.

Was Gabe paying her five hundred dollars a week because she earned it? Or was he making sure she had enough money that she wouldn't have any excuse not to leave when her six months at the Crested-C Ranch were over?

If her past had any bearing on her future, Sara feared she already knew the answer to that question.

AFTER SARA LEFT, Gabe let out a worried sigh. He'd tried his best to make Sara feel welcome. He'd even thought he was making some progress. But their conversation proved he had a long way to go before he convinced Sara that she and Ben belonged in Redstone.

Not that he could really blame her.

She'd been betrayed her entire life.

And in a way, Gabe knew he was betraying her, too.

He was urging her to meet friends and start feeling like she belonged. Yet, at the same time he was still allowing Sara to think whatever she wanted about his relationship with Ronnie Kincaid.

He wasn't proud of it.

He knew he should have explained about Ronnie when Sara arrived at the ranch. But one thing held him back. Ronnie was an obstacle that kept the distance between him and Sara.

As long as Sara believed he was involved with Ronnie, Gabe knew he was safe. And as long as Sara kept her distance, Gabe knew there would be no opportunity to slip up and act on the physical attraction he felt for her.

Physical attraction was one thing.

But being a real husband to Sara was another.

His parents had been a shining example of what a marriage should be. They'd loved each other completely, body and soul. He simply didn't have it in him to offer that kind of love to any woman.

He'd offered Sara a home and security. He'd be

her friend. He'd be her protector. And he'd provide for her and Ben for as long as she would let him.

Responsibility, he could handle.

But that's where he had to draw the line.

Still, it couldn't hurt to have the Grahams come over to meet Sara and Ben, even though the idea had been Smitty's, not his. And thinking about Smitty took Gabe's thoughts back to the slight argument they'd had when Smitty first mentioned celebrating the Fourth of July at the Crested-C.

They'd been watching Ben ride his pony around the corral, Ben learning to handle the reins while one of the ranch hands named Slim held on to a tether to keep the pony under control. Gabe had made an innocent comment about how much Ben had learned in one short month. And Smitty had taken the opportunity to blindside Gabe.

"Yeah, Ben's learned a lot," Smitty had said. "Too bad he'll be leaving in five short months."

Gabe had known Smitty was baiting him.

But he'd been too afraid Sara had said something not to ask, "Has Sara said something to you about leaving?"

"Nope. But if you keep ignoring that little gal you married, I guarantee you she'll leave."

"I haven't been ignoring her," Gabe had argued. "Sara and I have a business deal, not a real marriage. And we both agreed that's all we'll ever have."

Smitty snorted. "And that's what you think it takes to keep a woman happy? A business deal?"

"Keeping Sara happy wasn't part of the deal," Gabe had been quick to remind him.

"You're wrong. Keeping people happy is always part of any deal. Say you sell a man a horse, for instance. But he calls you later and says he isn't happy with the horse you sold him. If you're a good businessman you'll do whatever it takes to make him happy with the horse he has. Or you'll offer him a new deal."

"I'm happy with the deal we have," Gabe had grumbled.

"But the key is keeping Sara happy with the deal you have. If you're not willing to be a real husband to her, then you'd better be sure she makes some friends so she'll have a good reason to stay."

Gabe had been searching for a comeback when Smitty said, "I think we should invite the Grahams over for the Fourth of July this year. It's time Sara and Ben met their neighbors."

But as Gabe rose behind his desk and headed to bed, he couldn't help but be a little worried that forcing Sara to meet their neighbors was pushing her too fast. He'd seen the panicked look in her eyes when he first mentioned inviting the Grahams.

His only consolation was knowing he could count on Joe and Betsy to accept Ben and Sara without question. Joe had been his best friend since they were kids. Gabe had been Joe's best man when he and Betsy got married right out of high school.

Of course, they hadn't spent much time together since high school, him being single, them a married couple who later had a child. But now that Ben and Sara were part of his life, Gabe was actually looking forward to merging the two families.

Friends, Gabe thought, praying Smitty was right.

Maybe friends would give Sara a good reason to stay.

CHAPTER ELEVEN

"THIS IS my new friend, Junior, Mom," Ben said, and pushed a red-haired, freckle-faced boy in Sara's direction.

"And I'm five years old, too," Junior announced with a wide-toothed grin.

Sara stepped out onto the front porch.

She'd walked to the door when she first heard the truck pull up. But she'd been waiting while Ben bombarded their visitors with a dozen questions before they could even get out of the truck.

"I'm glad to meet you, Junior," Sara said, reaching down to shake the small hand she was being offered.

When she looked up, a woman with the same striking red hair was hurrying in her direction. She was tall, skinny as a rail, and her short hair framed her pretty face in a halo of red curls befitting a cherub.

"And I'm Betsy Graham, Junior's mother."

Before Sara could say hello, Betsy grabbed her

in a bear hug and gave Sara a healthy squeeze. "I just can't tell you how glad we are to have you and Ben in Redstone, Sara," she said. "Hardly a day goes by that Junior doesn't complain about not having a boy his own age to play with."

"Well, thank you, Betsy," Sara managed, completely overwhelmed by the woman's enthusiasm.

Betsy put her hands on her slim hips, looked over at Sara and rolled her eyes. Then she called out to the man who was heading around the house to where the picnic tables were set up, and where Gabe and the ranch hands were already busy playing horseshoes.

"Joe!" she yelled. "Act like you have some manners and come say hello to Sara before you head off with the boys."

He stopped mid-stride, turned and started back toward the porch. His physique was that of a football linebacker, but something about him told Sara his attitude was all teddy bear. He removed his cowboy hat as he walked up the steps, revealing sandy-blond hair beginning to thin on top. And the deep crinkles around his eyes said he smiled much more often than he frowned.

Sara liked him immediately.

"Nice to meet you, Sara," he said.

Sara briefly shook his hand.

"Don't even think about picking up a horseshoe

until you unload the truck and take the cooler and the other stuff we brought out back," Betsy said.

Joe put on his hat, looked at Sara and grinned. "You'll have to excuse me, Sara. As you can see, my bossy wife just gave me a direct order."

"I think you mean your beautiful, sexy, intelligent, bossy wife," Betsy teased. "And don't you forget it."

He gave Betsy a quick kiss on the lips and headed off.

The love between them was obvious. In spite of herself, Sara felt envious.

She quickly turned her attention to the boys. "I made some cookies this morning," Sara announced. "Do you boys know anyone who wants to sample them for me?"

"We do!" Ben and Junior yelled in unison.

The boys bolted through the front door, and Sara ushered her first official guest into the large Coulter kitchen—a comfortable get-to-know-you-better place. As she followed Betsy, Sara couldn't keep from thinking that just a little over a month ago her playing hostess to a Fourth of July picnic would have been as unbelievable as being called to the White House as an advisor for a world peace conference.

Yet, here she was.

And, surprisingly, not as nervous as she imagined.

"Smitty said you'd scrubbed everything around

here from top to bottom, Sara," Betsy said over her shoulder. "But girl, what you've done with this place is nothing short of a miracle."

Sara smiled, as Betsy made herself at home and flopped down at the kitchen table with the boys. She licked her finger and wiped a smidge of dirt from the tip of Junior's nose before she said, "You've got this place looking like it did back when Gabe's mother was alive. I bet Mary is shouting your praises from heaven at this very moment."

Sara's smile instantly faded.

A lifetime of always being on the outside looking in caused Sara to say, "I think we both know it isn't likely Mary Coulter would ever sing my praises in heaven, Betsy."

A splash of pink instantly dotted Betsy's cheeks.

She reached out without asking and took two of Sara's cookies from the plate on the table. "Why don't you boys take your cookies outside," Betsy suggested, "and go see those new puppies Ben was telling us about."

When the boys dashed out, Betsy wasted no time saying, "Look, Sara, you obviously took that remark wrong, and—"

"Surely you realize why I'm on the defensive here. I'm not stupid, Betsy. I know the whole town is talking about Gabe only marrying me so he could bring his nephew home."

Betsy's face turned solemn. "Maybe I'm the one who should be on the defensive, Sara. You've obviously already made up your mind about me. But if you think I've shown up to get a good look at the woman who had Billy Coulter's illegitimate son, I hate to disappoint you. The only reason I'm here is because we both have boys the same age and I hoped we might become good friends."

Sara opened her mouth to apologize.

But she burst into tears instead.

In a flash, Betsy was by her side with her arm around Sara's shoulder. "You go ahead and cry," Betsy said, giving Sara's back a supportive pat. "I'm sure it's a luxury you haven't allowed yourself stuck out here with a bunch of men."

Betsy ushered Sara to a chair, then took a seat beside her.

"I'm so embarrassed," Sara said, using the hem of her apron to wipe her eyes. "And I'm so sorry for doubting why you came."

"Oh, pooh," Betsy said. "No reason to be embarrassed or sorry. Who wouldn't feel like crying in your situation? You're in a strange house. In a strange town—"

"Married to a strange man," Sara said absently.

Betsy laughed. "Well, *strange* is an appropriate word to describe Gabe, I guess, but he's a good man. And I think you already know that or you and Ben wouldn't be here."

"I didn't mean Gabe was strange," Sara said, dabbing at her eyes again. "I meant we're basically strangers. But you're right, Betsy. Gabe is a good man. And he's totally committed to Ben."

Betsy looked at her knowingly for a moment. "You just always pictured the man you married being totally committed to *you.* Right?"

"Something like that."

Betsy patted Sara's hand. "Well, if it's any consolation, no one around here gives a hoot how you and Gabe ended up together. You and Ben are Gabe's family now. And everyone in town is dying to meet you."

When Sara sent Betsy a doubtful look, Betsy said, "And if that look has anything to do with Ronnie Kincaid, then I wouldn't waste my time worrying about her if I were you."

Sara opened her mouth to deny it.

"There aren't any secrets in a small town, Sara. Everyone in Redstone knows everyone else's business. Ronnie's been chasing Gabe since she got her first training bra. If Gabe had wanted to marry her, he would have done so a long time ago. Ronnie knows it. And so does everyone else."

Sara felt a huge weight lift from her shoulders.

"Thanks for telling me that, Betsy. I've felt so guilty worrying that Gabe sacrificed his own plans for Ben."

Betsy patted her hand again. "I've known Gabe all my life. Gabe Coulter never does anything he doesn't want to do. You're here because he wants you and Ben here."

Sara didn't know what to say.

But she was saved from saying anything when Junior suddenly burst through the kitchen door with a wiggling black puppy clasped firmly in both hands. Right behind him was Ben. And right behind Ben was a nervous-looking Bess, unsure of the little stranger who was holding her pup.

"Look what Ben gave me, Mama." Junior beamed. "I'm gonna name him Charcoal."

Sara and Betsy both laughed.

And Sara realized she and Ben had just made their first new friends in Redstone.

GABE STOOD ALONE later that night, sipping a beer and watching the small group sitting around the campfire on the benches they'd dragged over from the picnic tables. Smitty was busy helping Ben and Junior load up their roasting sticks with more marshmallows. Joe and Betsy were sitting together, Joe's arm around Betsy's shoulder.

Then there was Sara, sitting on a bench by herself, her own roasting stick and marshmallow held over the fire.

Sara laughed at something Betsy said, and it made Gabe realize how long it had been since laughter or having friends over had been a part of his daily life on the Crested-C. Fifteen years to be exact—too long.

Of course, that hadn't been the case when his parents were alive. His mother hadn't been in her element unless she was surrounded with friends and busy putting out food for those friends to enjoy.

His gaze returned to Sara.

She was a lot like his mother in many ways.

Sara was easy to be around, always making sure everyone else was taken care of. She'd been nothing but gracious to the Grahams. Just as she'd made all of the preparations for the day seem effortless.

But he shouldn't have been staring at her. Sara sensed it and looked up.

And though Gabe told himself to head for the card game going on in the bunkhouse, he found himself walking in her direction. He shocked both of them when he sat down on the bench right beside her.

She moved over slightly.

And Gabe sat up a little straighter.

"Get Gabe a stick and a marshmallow," Betsy

said to Joe, somewhat defusing the awkward moment.

"No, thanks," Gabe said, holding up his bottle. "Beer and marshmallows don't mix very well."

"You big wimp," Betsy scoffed. But she looked directly at Sara and said, "In case you haven't figured it out, Sara, Gabe isn't a risk taker. He never does anything even remotely risky."

"That isn't true," Gabe said, slightly embarrassed.

"Oh, pooh," Betsy said. "Of course, it's true. Name one thing you've ever done in your entire life that was risky."

Marrying Sara and keeping my hands off her?

Out loud Gabe said, "Our senior year. You and Joe dared me to jump Clayton's Gulch with Ricky Smith's motorcycle and I did it."

Betsy rolled her eyes and looked at Sara again. "Clayton's Gulch is a ten-foot ravine just outside of town where the teenagers still hang out and party. And yes, Gabe did jump the gulch on Ricky Smith's motorcycle when Joe and I dared him. But he'd seen Ricky jump that gulch a million times and he already knew it was possible. So I don't call that taking a risk."

"Gabe still had the balls to do it," Joe said.

"Joe!" Betsy scolded, elbowing Joe in the side as she nodded toward the other side of the campfire. "Watch your language in front of the boys."

"Dammit, that hurt," Joe grumbled.

Gabe and Sara both laughed.

"Okay, Betsy. You've tried to shame me. So tell us something risky you've done that can *top* jumping Clayton's Gulch," Gabe taunted.

Betsy grinned. "I can top jumping Clayton's Gulch hands down. Joe and I had steamy sex once on the sofa in the living room while my parents were home upstairs."

Joe frowned. "Hey! What happened to watching our language around the boys?"

Sara laughed.

But Gabe didn't.

Not with Sara sitting so close.

And not with *steamy sex* floating through his mind.

He stood, looked at Joe and quickly changed the subject. "I came over to tell you the boys are playing poker for money tonight. Want to help me take some of that money?"

Joe automatically looked over at Betsy for an answer.

"Oh, go on," Betsy said, and pushed Joe toward Gabe.

Thanks. I needed that reality check, Gabe thought.

He'd been in a strange mood all day. One minute, wondering what it would be like if he and Sara did have a real marriage. The next minute, worried that he'd even had such a troubling thought. But seeing Joe just now, waiting for permission from his wife to walk twenty yards to play cards, made Gabe realize he would *never* be husband material.

No way.

No how.

Not in this lifetime.

WHEN GABE AND JOE walked off, Betsy smiled at Sara. "I think your husband has a big crush on you."

"Betsy!" Sara protested. It was her turn to nod toward Smitty and the boys, who were now totally entranced by the sparklers Smitty had bought for them.

"What?" Betsy demanded. "You and Gabe *are* married, you know."

"Only on paper," Sara said.

"Oh, pooh." Betsy snorted. "The sexual tension between you two is so thick you couldn't chop through it with a wood ax."

"You keep forgetting Gabe has a girlfriend to take care of his sexual tensions."

"Don't be so sure about that," Betsy said. "I hear Ronnie's foreman is sharing her bed at the moment."

"I couldn't care less," Sara lied. "About Gabe or Ronnie. And especially what bed they're sharing."

"That is such a lie, Sara. And I don't care what

you say, Gabe does have a crush on you. I've watched him all day. His eyes get all dreamy every time he looks at you.

Sara laughed. "Now *that* is such a lie!"

But she couldn't keep from wishing it were true.

She'd thoroughly enjoyed having the Grahams over. She liked playing hostess. She'd even enjoyed the fantasy that they were a real couple even though she'd promised herself she'd never fantasize about Gabe Coulter again.

But she just couldn't help it. Gabe really was her cowboy dream come true.

Reality, after all, could always wait until tomorrow.

CHAPTER TWELVE

SINCE THE FOURTH of July party, mealtime had become the only time Sara saw Gabe. According to Smitty, July was one of the busiest months on the ranch, but something told her Gabe had been avoiding her the past three weeks on purpose. And that reminded Sara of what Betsy had told her about there being no secrets in a small town.

Was Gabe upset over Ronnie's alleged affair?

Or was Ronnie upset over Gabe's party?

Whatever the reason, Sara suspected they were feuding. And that's why she'd asked Gabe if she could talk to him a few minutes after Ben was in bed. He'd looked surprised at her request. But he'd agreed to wait for her in his office after she got Ben settled.

Now, Ben was settled.

And Sara was still standing at the top of the stairs, rehearsing what she planned to say and dreading every minute of it. She finally took a deep breath and descended before she lost her nerve. Gabe looked up from his computer the minute she walked into his office.

Sara took a seat in front of his desk.

Gabe smiled slightly, but his expression was pensive.

Sara got right to the point. "Betsy wants me to help her with a fund-raising booth at the Founder's Day celebration in town next weekend."

He let out a loud sigh of relief, and hit Sara with a wide grin. "Is that all you wanted to talk to me about? Sorry, but you had me worried something was seriously wrong."

"That's what I'm hoping to avoid," Sara said.

He looked puzzled this time.

"I'm hoping to avoid something going wrong if I do decide to help Betsy at Founder's Day."

He laughed, still not getting her drift. "You don't have to worry about anything going wrong with Betsy in charge. She's been on the Founder's Day committee forever. All the proceeds go to Redstone's volunteer fire department and Joe's the volunteer fire captain. There are a lot of nice people you haven't met yet, Sara. I'm glad you're willing to help Betsy. You and Ben will have a great time."

"And what about the not-so-nice people in Redstone?"

Sara knew the second he finally got it. His eyes turned a deeper shade of blue.

"Your personal life is none of my business, Gabe," Sara said. "But I hope you understand why I'm worried that Ben could be subjected to another temper tantrum from your girlfriend. Before I tell Betsy I'll help her, I want your guarantee there won't be any trouble from Ronnie."

"Sara," he said. "Maybe it's time we had a talk about Ronnie."

He stood and walked around his desk.

But his voice had suddenly gone all soft.

And the look in his eyes was, well, dreamy.

Sara popped out of her chair like a jack-in-the-box. She was not up to hearing talk about that woman—not when Sara herself still hadn't shaken those silly dreams where Gabe rode the white stallion and rescued her.

"Anyway, that's all I wanted to say," Sara said, quickly backing toward the door. "I just wanted to warn you that Betsy was trying to recruit me. You know. So you could ward off any conflict if Ben and I do go into town."

Sara kept retreating.

Gabe kept advancing.

She could already smell him—fresh hay and leather—and the scent was so intoxicating it almost made her swoon. Her back bumped the doorjamb, and Sara flattened herself against it. He was standing much too close for comfort. One step closer and she'd have her arms around his neck and her fingers tangled in his sun-streaked hair.

He kept looking at her.

Sara kept holding her breath.

"I should have explained about Ronnie a long time ago," he said, "but I—"

"I'm not asking you for an explanation, Gabe. Like I said, your personal life is none of my business. I'm only asking you to keep Ronnie away from Ben. And I don't think that's an unreasonable request."

Sara could tell Gabe wanted to say something else.

But he didn't.

And Sara saw her chance. She hurried through the door to safety. But when she reached the stairs, Sara looked over her shoulder to find Gabe still in his office doorway. "I told Betsy I would give her an answer," Sara said. "I'd appreciate you clearing things with Ronnie as soon as possible."

Gabe nodded and walked into his office.

And Sara's heart sank.

How badly she'd wanted him to come after her. How desperately she'd wanted him to say it was over with Ronnie and that Sara had nothing to worry about.

But he didn't.

Just as she would never tell Gabe how she really

felt about him. Or that the very thought of him being with Ronnie Kincaid made Sara crazy. That *her* bed was where he belonged. And that no one would ever love him as much or appreciate him more than she already did.

ONLY MINUTES AFTER Sara went upstairs, Gabe lingered outside her bedroom, his hand poised for a gentle knock. He'd come to finally tell Sara the truth about Ronnie. He was only one second away from knocking. But, instead, Gabe's arm fell to his side.

If Sara opened the door, there'd be no going back. She'd know about Ronnie and that would eliminate the one solid obstacle between him and Sara. There would be no reason the two of them couldn't turn this marriage into a true one.

And Gabe couldn't help it, but he just wasn't ready.

Not for love.

Love was a risky business. Love left a man wide open. Disrupted his focus. Kept him off balance. Handing his heart over to Sara could very well result in her throwing it right back in his face. And that was a risk he just wasn't ready to take.

She'd told him only moments ago that his personal life was none of her business. That she didn't want an explanation about his relationship with Ronnie. And though instinct told him that wasn't necessarily honest, Gabe had to take her words at face value.

Better to leave things the way they were.

Honor the agreement they'd made, and stick to it.

His decision made, Gabe stepped back from the door and headed down the hallway for his nightly check on Ben. Gabe had already decided that he would talk to Ronnie as Sara had asked him to do.

Sara wasn't the only one who had no interest in having Ben subjected to Ronnie's wrath. And though Gabe hadn't even seen Ronnie since the day he brought Ben and Sara home, he'd make sure Ronnie knew that his warning to leave his family alone hadn't been an idle threat.

Ben and Sara were under his care now.

Coulters took care of their own.

CHAPTER THIRTEEN

TWO MONTHS AFTER Sara and Ben's arrival in Colorado, the Coulters left the Crested-C for their first official outing as a family. Smitty had gone on ahead to Redstone with the rest of the ranch hands in Gabe's truck.

"You'll have to take the *family* vehicle to Founder's Day," Smitty had teased Gabe at breakfast. "I need your truck to haul the boys."

He'd been referring, of course, to Sara's new red Jeep Cherokee.

Sitting behind the wheel of the Jeep now, Gabe could have passed for the typical family man, Sara supposed. Except for the fact that this family man also had a girlfriend. A girlfriend who, according to Gabe, had been prewarned that he was taking his new family to the celebration.

Still, Sara couldn't keep from being nervous about running into Ronnie again. And the steep gravel road leading down the mountain from the ranch wasn't helping the queasiness in her stomach one bit.

"Junior's gonna show me all the fun things to do," Ben announced from the backseat. "He's been to Founder's Day before."

Sara turned sideways in her seat. "That's fine, Ben. As long as you stay where I can see you."

"Aw, Mom," Ben grumbled, prompting Gabe to laugh.

"You're forgetting you can practically see from one end of Redstone to the other, Sara," Gabe spoke up in Ben's defense.

"It still doesn't hurt to be careful," Sara said. "Ben hasn't lived here all his life. He doesn't know his way around town yet."

"Do, too," Ben argued. "Me and Smitty's walked all over that town, Mom."

"Smitty and I," Sara corrected. As far as she was concerned, the subject was closed.

Of course, Ben getting lost in Redstone was the least of her worries. She'd tried to take Betsy's words of encouragement that Gabe wouldn't let Ronnie cause a scene to heart. But another run-in with the woman had never been far from Sarah's mind. How did the pretend wife address the girlfriend who had a legitimate claim to the man's affection? Not something any of Sara's experience had prepared her for.

And so Sara forced herself to ask, "What about you, Gabe? Where will you be while I'm helping Betsy, and Junior's showing Ben all the fun things to do in town?"

"Close at hand."

You'd better be close at hand.

"Betsy never actually told me what she wanted me to do to help her. What type of fund-raising booths do they have?"

Gabe shrugged. "The usual, I guess. Some booths have arts and crafts. There's always plenty of food. And there are some carnival-type booths where the kids can try their luck at winning prizes."

"And I'm gonna win lotsa prizes," Ben declared.

Gabe laughed and said, "Did you bring your allowance, Ben? You have to pay to play the games."

Ben grinned and held up his two ten-dollar bills.

Sara had never been to a Founder's Day celebration. But it did sound like something she would enjoy. And that's exactly what she intended to do. She was going to enjoy herself and have fun without worrying that something bad was going to happen.

Maybe all the worrying was the real problem anyway. She had a bad habit of expecting the worst. And the worst was usually what happened to her. Maybe it was time to expect nothing but the good.

Bring on the good.

It would be a welcome change from a lifetime of bad.

GABE KNEW exactly why Sara had asked where he planned to be during Founder's Day—the same reason he'd made a trip to the Flying-K earlier in the week. He'd told Ronnie he was taking Ben and Sara to Founder's Day, and he'd warned her she'd better not start any trouble.

"Don't flatter yourself," she'd snapped.

But now, Gabe worried his visit had only been the equivalent of waving a red flag in front of a bull. Ronnie never took any slight—real or imagined—lying down. And that meant he'd keep an eye on Ben and Sara just in case. What he wanted most was for Sara and Ben to have a good time, to feel like they belonged in this town.

He glanced at Sara again, noticing for the first time she was wearing a hint of makeup today. The mascara emphasized her long, dark eyelashes, and a touch of pink lipstick made her lips look full and moist.

She glanced over at him.

For once, Gabe said exactly what he was thinking. "You look exceptionally pretty today, Sara. Doesn't she, Ben?"

"Mom always looks pretty," Ben said.

"I agree."

She blushed slightly.

"Well, thank you both," she said, reaching up to push a few wisps of hair under her hair clasp.

Gabe turned his attention to the road, pleased with himself that he could pay Sara a compliment, she could accept it, and that was that. No expectations, no declarations of undying love, just a simple observation. He'd been able to get a grip on his emotions over the past week after that close call of almost knocking on Sara's bedroom door.

And what a mistake that would have been.

Sara didn't need him sending her mixed signals—not when he wasn't ready to offer her anything other than the friendship he promised. He'd let his emotions temporarily override his own common sense. But now he was back in control, and Gabe intended to keep it that way.

He'd weathered the storm and he'd come through, his old self again. And the fact that Sara had agreed to go to Founder's Day led him to believe she was finally beginning to be comfortable with him and their arrangement. Just as he was feeling comfortable.

Sara and Betsy hitting it off so well was even more assurance that Sara seemed to be settling in. And he was definitely glad Ben and Junior had become best friends. Kids needed other kids around, an escape from the adults who looked after them. Gabe wouldn't trade anything for his boyhood days. He hoped one day Ben would look back on his childhood and feel the same way.

Yes, things did seem to be falling into place.

Sara and Ben had friends to keep them happy.

And Gabe had a ranch to run.

Life was good.

Gabe drove into Redstone and the first person they saw was Betsy waving madly in their direction. She held Junior's hand as Gabe pulled the Cherokee up beside them.

"Redstone Boulevard's blocked off and Joe's gone ahead to find a parking place," Betsy said. "I was hoping you'd let Sara out here with me. It'll save time and we need to beat the crowd to our booth."

"Sure," Gabe said, looking over at Sara. "Go on with Betsy. Ben and Junior can go with me to park the Jeep. We'll find Joe and catch up with you later."

Sara sent him a worried look.

And Gabe realized maybe Sara wasn't as comfortable with him as he'd hoped. For reassurance, he said, "I'd never let anything happen to Ben. You know that."

Only then did she open her car door.

Trust, Gabe thought.

Slowly but surely Sara was beginning to trust him.

Provider.

Protector.

Friend.

Sara could count on him to be all those things.

GABE DROVE OFF with both boys and Sara found herself being dragged along by Betsy, who still hadn't bothered to tell her exactly what fund-raising booth needed her help so desperately.

"You look absolutely gorgeous, Sara," Betsy said. "All wholesome and sweet. Like a fresh summer day."

Sara laughed. "I'm sure you say that to all the victims you railroad into helping you."

But as they walked down Redstone Boulevard Sara realized even in her simple white eyelet cotton sundress she was still completely over-dressed for the occasion. Betsy and all of the other women she'd seen so far were wearing jeans.

"I do wish you'd warned me that I needed to wear jeans, though," Sara said, thinking out loud. "I'm starting to feel self-conscious in this dress."

"Oh, pooh," Betsy said. "You always wear dresses. I bet you don't even own a pair of jeans."

"But I could have bought a pair," Sara protested.

Betsy looked at her. "Seriously? You really don't own a pair of jeans?"

"I've always preferred dresses," Sara lied.

She didn't know Betsy well enough yet to tell her the hurtful things her foster mother had said when she threw Sara out because she was pregnant. That the self-righteous woman had accused Sara of being a low-life whore just like her mother. And that the woman had screamed at her, demanding to know what Sara expected walking around in skintight jeans and flaunting her body in front of men to get their attention.

Sara hadn't worn jeans since.

"I can't believe you don't own a pair of jeans," Betsy said, shaking her head in disbelief. "I'm sorry, Sara, but that's just plain *wrong*. You can't be a rancher's wife and not own jeans."

"I'll be sure to jot that down in my rancher's-wife handbook," Sara shot back.

Betsy laughed. "You do that. But honestly, you couldn't have dressed more appropriately for our fund-raising booth."

"What type of booth is it?" Sara quizzed.

An older couple approached, delaying an answer.

"Sara Coulter, I want you to meet Marge and Hank Jones," Betsy said. "Hank and Marge own Jones Country Store."

Being introduced as Sara Coulter for the first

time addled Sara for a moment, but she managed to nod and say a polite hello.

"Your Ben is just adorable, Sara," Marge told her. "And so polite. I told Smitty the other day how refreshing it was to see a boy Ben's age with nice manners." She winked at Sara. "Proof that he has a good mother."

"Why, thank you, Marge," Sara said.

Betsy waited until Hank and Marge walked on down the street before she looked over at Sara and said, "Good girl."

"Excuse me?"

"I'm bragging on you for accepting Marge's compliment without reading anything into it," Betsy said. "It gives me hope you might eventually lose that Princess of Paranoia tiara you've been wearing."

Old habits die hard, Sara thought.

Out loud she said, "Oh, pooh!" stealing Betsy's favorite expression.

They both laughed.

Until Betsy came to a stop.

"Here we are," Betsy announced happily.

Sara felt the blood drain to her feet.

The booth had two giant red lips painted on the front.

The sign below the lips read: Kisses $10.00.

"Okay, cutie, now get behind the counter and

make us lots of money," Betsy said. "I'll round up the business and collect the money. You pucker up and deliver some smoking-hot kisses."

Sara remained glued to the spot.

"Oh, no, you don't. Don't you dare read anything into why I asked you to help me. I didn't even know which booth we'd get until this week."

"And I've talked to you or seen you every day this week," Sara reminded her, "and not once did you mention anything about a kissing booth."

"Would you have helped if I had mentioned it?"

"Absolutely not."

"And that's exactly why I didn't tell you," Betsy admitted with a grin.

The look Sara sent her said she wasn't appeased.

"Okay, Sara, I apologize for not telling you. But this kissing booth is a town tradition the mayor insists we include every year no matter how much anyone protests. Back when Redstone was first founded, women were scarce. The only chance most cowboys had to get a kiss was at the Founder's Day booth."

"You people sure are big on tradition," Sara grumbled.

"You bet we're big on tradition," Betsy said. "But do you know how much money the kissing booth made last year?" Betsy answered her own question. "Twenty lousy dollars. We've tried to explain to the mayor that cowboys aren't going to hand over their hard-earned money to kiss a bunch of women they've known since the cradle. And that's another reason I didn't tell you so you could back out. With a pretty new face like yours I guarantee we're going to need a wheelbarrow to haul off all our money at the end of the day."

"No, we're going to need the wheelbarrow to haul off your dead body," Sara threatened.

"You can kill me after we make tons of money," Betsy promised. "The fire department needs new hoses for the truck and those hoses don't come cheap."

"And if I refuse?"

Betsy looked at Sara for a long time. "Then you'll be missing a great opportunity to show everyone in town that you're a good sport, Sara. And that you're willing to do your part in your new community."

When Sara didn't answer, Betsy said, "Come on, Sara. What's the harm in giving a few cowboys a kiss on the cheek?"

"Only on the cheek?"

"Only on the cheek," Betsy assured her. She slid her purse off her shoulder, fished inside and handed Sara a compact and a tube of lipstick. "Bright red," Betsy said, "to match the lips on the sign. Now lather up those lips and get ready to make us some money."

Before Sara could argue, Betsy started yelling to the crowd of people walking up and down the street. "Kisses. Come get your kisses, cowboys. Ten dollars gets you a kiss from the prettiest lips in Redstone."

Sara groaned and rolled her eyes.

But she lathered her lips just as Betsy instructed.

A nicely dressed man was the first one to walk up and stop in front of their booth. His three-piece suit was nicely pressed and his silver hair was impeccably groomed. He was sixty-something, a little on the chubby side, and he had the perpetual smile of a lifelong politician.

It didn't really surprise Sara when Betsy slapped him on the back and said, "This is our mayor, Gordon Cooper, Sara. Mayor Cooper is always the first customer in line at the kissing booth on Founder's Day."

Sara smiled at the man and said hello.

She noticed people were now gathering around the booth at a mind-spinning pace. Several people even clapped when the mayor reached into the pocket of his vest and produced a crisp ten-dollar bill. He closed his eyes, leaned forward and, to Sara's horror, produced an absolutely perfect pucker.

"Go for it, Gordon!" someone yelled out.

That's when Sara noticed Gabe standing at the back of the crowd, a big fat grin on his face at her predicament. She'd asked him point-blank what types of booths she could expect at Founder's Day. And not once had he mentioned anything about the town's traditional kissing booth.

So Gabe thinks this is funny, does he?

Sara placed her hands on both sides of the Mayor Cooper's chubby cheeks and kissed the poor man so thoroughly she feared he might need the assistance of the volunteer fire department to resuscitate him when she finally let him go. No one said a word when the mayor practically staggered away from the booth.

Then one cowboy yelled, "Hot damn! I'm next."

Within seconds, cowboys from every direction began falling in line. When Sara looked back at Gabe his big grin was gone. Seconds later, so was he.

Oh, no. What have I done? It was her first official appearance in town, and she'd obviously embarrassed Gabe thoroughly. *Plus* she'd almost given Redstone's mayor a coronary.

"What part of *cheek* did you not understand?" Betsy leaned over and whispered. "We're close to having a stampede on our hands here."

"It was Gabe's *cheeky* grin," Sara whispered

back. "He was laughing at me. And I'm sorry, but it made me furious."

"Jeez," Betsy said. "I wish you two would just jump each other's bones and get it over with."

"Betsy!"

But Betsy turned back to face the rowdy crowd and do a little damage control. "Sorry, boys," she said with a big grin, "but the rest of you only get a kiss on the cheek. Only Mayor Cooper qualifies for lip service, since that's what Gordon gives us most of the time."

Everybody laughed.

But not a single cowboy fell out of line.

CHAPTER FOURTEEN

COWBOY AFTER COWBOY took any type of kiss Sara was willing to give them before they strolled off down the street, an imprint of her bright red lips on their cheeks, and a big smile on their faces. Betsy was happy raking in the money. The crowd cheered the cowboys on. Sara was even getting caught up in the merriment.

Until her worst nightmare became a reality.

From out of nowhere, Ronnie Kincaid slithered up to join the rest of the curious onlookers, a far-from-friendly smile on her face. Everything about the woman screamed sex appeal. Black silk shirt, unbuttoned to show her cleavage. Black skintight jeans and black high-heeled boots. Pouting lips. Bedroom eyes.

She could have been featured in an X-rated movie.

And there stood Sara, looking like Mary Poppins.

Call her the Princess of Paranoia, but Sara knew it wasn't her imagination that everyone kept looking at Ronnie, then back at her. They were comparing the dowdy wife to the sex-kitten girlfriend. And it didn't take a genius to figure out who was winning most of the votes.

Ronnie moved a little closer to the booth.

Sara stood a little straighter.

Her first instinct was to call out to Ben, who was running across the street with Junior to join a group of other children. But she thought better of it when Ronnie's cold gaze narrowed in her direction. Better if Ben were safely on the other side of the street, Sara quickly decided, when another glance around the crowd proved that Mr. Close-at-Hand was still nowhere to be found.

Sara managed to smile at the cowboy who had just handed over his money, but she continued to watch her enemy out of the corner of her eye. And Ronnie was sure laying it on thick—mingling here and there, strutting her stuff, laughing a bit too loudly.

She was definitely up to something.

It didn't calm Sara's nerves when a good-looking cowboy walked up beside Ronnie and threw his arm possessively around her shoulder. Betsy had mentioned she heard Ronnie was seeing someone. But Sara suspected Ronnie was only trying to make Gabe jealous. And when Ronnie whispered something in the cowboy's ear that made him throw his head back and laugh, her suspicions were confirmed.

Gabe had brought his fake wife to town.

So Ronnie had decided to bring her fake boyfriend.

"Red alert," Betsy warned, as if Sara couldn't already see that for herself. "I think you'd better take a break until the storm blows by."

"Thank you," Sara said, and quickly stepped aside.

"Okay, boys," Betsy said. "I think it's time we gave this pretty lady a break. Pretty lips like hers aren't used to kissing scruffy faces. But I'm a hometown gal. Scruffy is all I know."

A groan of disapproval rumbled through the crowd.

"Forget it, Betsy," called one of the cowboys in line. "I'm not paying ten dollars to kiss somebody I kissed for free in sixth grade."

The crowd clapped and hollered at his comment.

"But I'm a much better kisser than I was in sixth grade, Jim," Betsy replied. "Step on up here and find out for yourself."

More laughs. More clapping.

Sara was beginning to think Betsy had saved the day.

"I'll pay one hundred dollars for a kiss from that

pretty brunette," the cowboy standing with Ronnie called out.

Everyone turned to look at him.

"French style," he added, looking Sara up and down with a leering grin. "Long and slow."

Nobody laughed this time.

But even more people began gathering around the booth. Waiting, Sara knew, for the fireworks to begin.

Damn you, Gabe Coulter, Sara thought at the exact same time an unexpected arm slid tightly around her waist.

"Are you deaf, Charlie?" Gabe called out to Ronnie's cohort. "My wife is taking a break."

It was so quiet Sara could hear her own heart beating.

"Maybe you should let your wife decide for herself if she's taking a break, Gabe?" he said with a satisfied smirk. "She might like it. From what I hear, she isn't even getting kissed over at the Crested-C."

Without warning Gabe pulled Sara to face him.

And he kissed her senseless.

It was a kiss filled with every ounce of passion she'd been trying to suppress. A kiss that made the world stop, the cheers from the rowdy crowd fade and time stand perfectly still.

When their lips parted, Gabe looked as shaken

as Sara felt. But he kept his arm tightly around her waist when he sent Ronnie's troublemaker another deadly look. "You heard wrong, Charlie," Gabe said. "But if you're still looking to get kissed today, I'd say your best bet is standing right beside you."

Sara felt her face flame.

Gabe had kissed her. But only to make Ronnie jealous.

Ronnie smacked Charlie's arm off her shoulder and stomped down the street, pushing people out of her way. Charlie only laughed and strolled after her.

Sara slowly eased out of Gabe's grasp. But she was way too angry to pretend that she wasn't.

Turning her back to the crowd, Sara snapped, "The next time you decide to make Ronnie jealous, Gabe, don't do it at my expense."

"I thought you said my personal life was none of your business."

"It isn't. As long as you don't put me in the middle."

"You're wrong, Sara," he said. "I was only trying to protect you."

"Protect me? Protecting me would have been making sure your girlfriend kept her word and didn't make a scene."

Anger flashed in his eyes again. Then he dug into the front pocket of his jeans and handed over the keys to the Cherokee. "I think it's best if I ride back with the boys. You and Ben can take the Cherokee."

"Gladly!" And she meant it.

Gabe walked away.

But nothing would ever be the same between them again.

Not after a kiss like that one.

CHARLIE GRABBED the driver's side door of the Suburban before Ronnie could slam it. "Let go of the damn door, Charlie," Ronnie warned. "I mean it."

She tried to pull it shut, but he was stronger.

"Move over," he said, giving her a push. "I drove you here. I'll drive you home."

Several people had already stopped to watch. Ronnie leveled a she-devil glare in their direction. They took the hint and hurried on down the street.

Only then did Ronnie give in and move over so Charlie could slide behind the wheel. But they were well out of Redstone before Charlie finally looked over at her.

"I'm the one who should be pissed off, you know," he said. "Gabe was ready to kick my ass back there."

Ronnie glared at him. "You could still get your ass kicked if you don't shut up."

He had the nerve to laugh.

"I hate it for you, babe," he taunted. "But if that kiss didn't prove how Gabe feels about his new wife, you need your vision checked."

"I said shut up!"

"And Gabe does have himself one fine-looking woman," Charlie rambled on. "No one can argue about that."

Ronnie made a lunge for him.

Charlie held her off with one hand.

"She's just not *my* type," he added.

"She's breathing, isn't she?" She flopped back against her seat in a huff.

"Yeah, she's breathing. And she'll probably be breathing pretty hard later tonight."

This time Ronnie's fist connected up against his jaw.

Again, Charlie only laughed at her.

"No, sir," he said. "Gabe's wife isn't my type at all." He sent Ronnie a smoldering look that left no doubt about what was on his mind. "No, I like my women bold and brassy. Hard to handle. You never know what to expect from a woman like that. But you can always guarantee one thing. The sex will be sizzling and leave you begging for more."

Their eyes locked for a second.

A white-hot heat spread through Ronnie like a flash fire. Charlie always knew exactly what to say to make her wet—get her hot—and make her want him.

Rough—no holding back.

That's the way she liked it.

And that's the way Charlie liked to give it to her.

He made a detour onto a dirt road leading down to the river. And by the time Charlie pulled the Suburban to a stop in a secluded area, Ronnie had forgotten all about Gabe giving his silly wife a stupid kiss. Charlie came at her the same way he always came at her, pulling her against him, devouring her mouth with his, taking her prisoner.

"Let's get in the back," Ronnie moaned when his tongue slid down her neck to lick the space between her breasts.

Minutes later she was naked and waiting for him on the folded-down backseat. He took his time climbing into the back of the truck, taunting her as he slowly unhooked his belt buckle. Finally, he let his jeans drop, giving Ronnie a good look at just how much he wanted her.

In one swift motion, he flipped her on her stomach.

Ronnie climaxed the second he plunged inside her.

CHAPTER FIFTEEN

IT WAS AFTER TEN on Sunday morning when Gabe tossed the last of his gear into the back of his truck. He'd skipped breakfast, in no mood to see Sara. And he'd spent the morning in the bunkhouse making a list of things he wanted done while he was gone. How long he'd be gone, Gabe wasn't sure. All he knew was that he had to put some distance between him and the woman who had his head all screwed up.

He still couldn't believe he'd lost control like that. Or that he'd actually been jealous over some damn silly kissing booth. But when every cowboy in the county started lining up to kiss Sara, he'd gone from jealous to outright pissed.

Then rage had taken over when Ronnie's foreman tried to harass Sara. Gabe should have just knocked Charlie out and put an end to it. Instead, Gabe had made a big mistake.

He'd kissed her.

Now there was no turning back.

At least not to the pretend existence he'd been trying to maintain since the day he brought Sara home. And that's what had him worried. Taking that giant step off the cliff called love scared the hell out of Gabe.

Chances were he'd never survive the fall.

"I never thought I'd see the day when someone else's horses were more important than your own," Smitty said as he limped in Gabe's direction.

Gabe's scowl didn't keep Smitty from lumbering up beside him. "I told you," Gabe said. "I'm just trying to help a friend out, that's all."

And part of his statement was true.

His good friend Rowdy Stancil had called a few days earlier complaining about a new stallion he couldn't quite break. Gabe had given Rowdy a few suggestions on the phone. But it wasn't until Gabe realized he was head over heels in love that he decided to pay Rowdy a visit in person.

"Rowdy ain't much of a friend, if you ask me," Smitty said, still trying, Gabe knew, to get a rise out of him before he left the ranch. "Nope. In my book, friends don't expect a man to run off and leave his crew shorthanded during the busiest time of the year."

Gabe ignored the comment and stomped to the driver's side. Smitty matched every step he took, despite the use of his cane. Once inside the cab, Gabe slammed the door and frowned at Smitty again.

"What's the matter, old man? You getting too frail to run this ranch without me?"

Smitty flashed a grin. "Are you too lovesick to stay and run this ranch yourself?"

Gabe frowned again, but he didn't bother to deny the accusation.

Gabe's only reply was to turn on the ignition and leave Smitty standing in a cloud of dust in the middle of the driveway.

Nosy old buzzard, Gabe thought, and picked up speed.

But it wasn't until he was miles away from the ranch that he finally relaxed his grip on the steering wheel and settled into his seat. What he needed was some good advice from his old friend Rowdy.

Some no-nonsense cowboy advice to be exact. And Rowdy was just the person to give it to him.

Rowdy always put his ranch first. He took his horses seriously, and there wasn't a female alive who had the power to tempt Rowdy Stencil into participating in some lovesick bullshit.

Love.

How could Gabe possibly be in love with someone he'd only known a couple of months? But he knew the answer before the question crossed his mind. He'd fallen in love with Sara the day she'd been standing at the picnic table in Texas, baring her soul and angry enough to cry.

But Rowdy will straighten me out.

Gabe put the pedal to the metal and headed for Montana.

Maybe they'd even take a few packhorses and head to the high country and get in a little trout fishing. Sleep out under the stars for a night or two. Get back to nature, where a man had the freedom to take a good look at his life and reaffirm his deepest beliefs. The same type of freedom a man lost when his heart got all tangled up with a woman who could render him defenseless with the turn of her head.

Gabe switched on the radio and a few minutes later he was whistling along to a lively country tune, still holding on to the firm belief that all it would take to clear his head was a little time away from the woman who had somehow managed to steal his heart.

SARA HAD WATCHED Gabe leave the ranch from the kitchen window. But it wasn't until Gabe's truck disappeared out of sight that she reacted. The sharp pain in her solar plexus nearly doubled her over.

Save the heartache, the voice inside her head had scolded. *Save it for when you have to explain to Ben why your decision to bring him to Colorado has blown up in your face.*

Sara straightened, pressed a hand to her midsection and called on her inner strength.

The same as she'd done at the kissing booth after the showdown with Ronnie. She'd stood there smiling like nothing was wrong and taking the money while Betsy took over handing out kisses. She'd refused to give Ronnie or Gabe the satisfaction of spoiling her son's first—and possibly last—Founder's Day celebration.

Gabe had not ventured far from their vicinity the rest of the day, even though he kept his distance. In fact, their only eye contact after the kiss had been the curt nod Gabe had given her when Ben took it upon himself to scamper off to tell his uncle they were leaving and heading for home.

Sara had secretly hoped Gabe would follow.

But he didn't.

Instead, it was much later when he'd returned to the ranch with Smitty and the ranch hands. She'd been tempted to knock on his bedroom door and tell him they needed to discuss the fiasco at the kissing booth but, of course, she hadn't done that, either.

She'd kept reassuring herself if she pretended the kiss had never happened, maybe Gabe would do the same. That maybe everything would blow over and things would return to normal.

But never once had Sara expected Gabe to

leave. If Gabe was willing to abandon the ranch during the busiest time of the year, there was no going back to normal. Clearly he was struggling with a decision.

He had a choice to make.

And Sara feared she knew what Gabe's choice would be.

Pack your things and leave now, she kept telling herself. But only one thing stopped her. She was not going to give Gabe Coulter an easy way out.

He'd been the one to storm into *their* lives, spouting clichés about blood kin and family ties. She and Ben certainly hadn't come looking for Gabe. He'd even challenged her to do what was best for her son.

So no, she wasn't going to leave.

She'd be right here when Gabe returned. And if it turned out Gabe wanted her and Ben gone, so be it. At least she could leave Redstone with a clear conscience, knowing she'd lived up to her end of the bargain.

"Got your shopping list ready?" Smitty more or less barked in Sara's direction as he opened the screen door and entered the kitchen.

Sara made her way to the opposite counter where the old guy knew full well she kept her running list of the supplies they needed. Personally, she thought Smitty's daily shopping trips were a big waste of time and money. And that they should buy in bulk for the ranch and stock supplies. But Sara also suspected without her daily list, Smitty would lose his excuse to spend most of his mornings in Redstone, hanging out with his cronies at Jones Country Store.

After handing him the list, Sara expected him to shuffle out of the kitchen the way he usually did. Instead, he poured himself a cup of coffee from the pot Sara always kept full, out of habit from her restaurant days. When he took a seat at the table, Sara retrieved the cream and sugar from the counter and placed them in front of him. He offered her a less than amicable grunt of thanks.

"It ain't none of my business how you run your kitchen, missy," Smitty said as he stirred the milk into his coffee. "But I've been meaning to mention that you'd save yourself a lot of time and hard work if you went back to using them paper plates and cups, and them plastic forks and spoons like I always used when I had to cook for the boys."

Sara held her temper in check, thinking to herself that Smitty would probably be back to using those paper plates and plastic forks much sooner than he expected. She said instead, "I guess it's just a woman thing, Smitty. With all the beautiful china and silverware in these cabinets, I think it would be a real shame not to use them."

"Mary wouldn't settle for anything but the very best," Smitty said with a hint of pride in his voice. "And Luke made sure the very best was what Mary had."

Aware that Smitty was obviously in the mood for a chat, Sara decided to take advantage of the situation. If anyone could give her any information about what was going on inside Gabe's head, Smitty could. But Sara knew she'd have to approach the subject cautiously, and only ask if Smitty gave her the opportunity.

She refreshed her own cup and took a seat beside the old man. "I don't mean to pry, Smitty," Sara began slowly, "but I've never known exactly what happened to Ben's grandparents."

He stirred his coffee a few more times before he answered. "It was a real tragedy. And that's a fact."

After a few more sips from his cup, Smitty said, "It was the middle of January fifteen years ago, but sometimes it seems like yesterday. Luke had taken Mary into town like he always did on Saturday mornings, and I kept the boys here with me to round up the livestock. There was a blizzard on the way and we had to get ready for it."

He looked at her and said, "You'll find out soon enough that snow is a fact of life at this elevation. When it starts flying it never stops. Not until spring."

Sara wasn't looking for a weather report—particularly since she might not be here come winter—but she knew better than to rush him.

Smitty heaved another deep sigh. "The weather bureau predicted the storm wouldn't reach Redstone until late Sunday night. But things turned real nasty by the time Luke and Mary started up the mountain that afternoon. Luke had driven these roads all his life, and I'm sure he thought he could make it. And he would have, if it hadn't already snowed so heavy on the mountain all that week.

"A small avalanche took out twenty feet of the road leading up to the ranch. And when it did, it swept Luke and Mary to the bottom of the canyon with it." He shook his head. "They were buried instantly. The snow was so deep it took two whole days to dig them out."

Sara shuddered, thinking how nervous she was traveling on the winding gravel road leading up to the Crested-C.

"Gabe was only eighteen," Smitty said, "and Billy was only eleven. But I watched Gabe Coulter become a man overnight. He took charge of this ranch, and he took care of his little brother. And he did a fine job of it, too."

"With a lot of help from you, I'm sure," Sara said, giving the old man credit where credit was due.

Smitty shrugged off her comment. "I was around in case Gabe needed me."

"But what about you, Smitty?" Sara decided to ask. "Don't you regret not having your own ranch and a family of your own?"

"Working this ranch is all I've ever needed," Smitty said with conviction.

Just like Gabe, Sara thought.

When Smitty's face suddenly turned grave with concern, Sara worried she'd actually said those words out loud.

"With Luke gone, I wasn't sure we could hold on to the ranch. A good breeder gets his business from a solid reputation, and at that point, Gabe wasn't much more than a snot-nosed kid. I ain't proud of it, but I pushed that boy day and night. And all the while I kept drilling it into Gabe's head that the ranch had to come first. That emotions were a sign of weakness. And that nothing or nobody could ever stand in his way if he wanted this ranch to be a success."

Sara reached out and touched his arm. "You did what you had to do, Smitty. And it worked."

"Yeah, it worked," Smitty said. "Maybe too good."

Before Sara could ask what he meant, Smitty cocked his head in her direction. "I don't mean to pry, either. But I can't for the life of me figure out why you let Gabe ride out of here this morning without telling that boy you were in love with him."

Sara blushed. "You mean it's that obvious?"

"To everyone but a stubborn fool like Gabe," Smitty said. "Don't you realize Gabe's running scared right now because he feels the same way about you?"

Sara was tempted to bring up the subject of Ronnie Kincaid, but her pride wouldn't let her go there. Instead, she said, "I do love Gabe, Smitty. But if Gabe feels the same way about me, he'll have to make the first move."

Smitty frowned and stroked his woolly beard. "You know," he said, "I had two old mules once that remind me a whole lot of you and Gabe."

Sara's eyebrows shot up a notch. "Oh, really?"

"One mule was so stubborn it wouldn't eat a bite, no matter what type of grain I tried to feed it. And the other mule wouldn't drink a drop of water, no matter how many times I led it to the trough to drink. I'm telling you, those two mules were a real sad pair. And that's a fact."

"So?" Sara asked on cue. "What did you do?"

"I shot them both and put them out of their misery."

Sara laughed. "And the moral to this story would be?"

The old man pushed himself back from the table and reached for his cane. At the door, he looked over his shoulder. "Life's too short to waste it being stubborn, missy. If you love Gabe, you tell him you love him before it's too late."

The screen door banged and Smitty was gone.

But Sara remained sitting at the table, staring into her cup and praying with all her heart that what Smitty said was true—Gabe was only running scared because he loved her, too.

CHAPTER SIXTEEN

GABE REACHED the Beartooth Ranch on the outskirts of Billings, Montana, just before nine o'clock Sunday night. The ten-hour-plus trip should have exhausted him. Instead, Gabe felt pumped up and ready for a little hell-raising. And he was counting on his old friend to oblige him.

Raising hell was how Rowdy got his nickname.

Gabe brought the truck to a stop in Rowdy's driveway, unconcerned that there were no lights on inside the house. Monday morning always started at sunrise. And like most cowboys, Rowdy restricted his partying to Friday and Saturday nights only.

Except on special occasions. And this Sunday night was one of those times.

Gabe left the truck and took a long, leisurely stretch before he bounded up the front-porch stairs and banged his fist against Rowdy's front door. It took several moments before a light came on, flashing a golden shadow across the front porch.

Gabe grinned and banged on the door even harder.

"Hold your horses, dammit! I'm coming," Rowdy yelled as he jerked the door open.

He stumbled onto the porch wearing nothing but the pair of jeans he was still trying to fasten at his waist. A big grin spread across his face when he realized who was banging on his front door.

"Why, Gabe Coulter, you old dog," Rowdy said. He gave Gabe's hand a firm shake. "Why didn't you let me know you were headed this way?"

"I've never needed an invitation before," Gabe said, and walked in past Rowdy without being invited. But he'd no sooner stepped inside the door when another voice rang out from the darkened hallway on Gabe's right.

"Rowdy, honey? Is everything okay?"

Gabe glanced at Rowdy. Rowdy shrugged and sent Gabe a sheepish grin.

"You go on back to bed now, sugar," he crooned to the redhead hovering outside his bedroom door. "Gabe's an old friend of mine from Colorado."

Gabe couldn't believe it. He'd known Rowdy most of his life. And the one rule Rowdy had always lived by was "never take a woman to your own bed unless you plan to keep her there on a permanent basis."

Not Rowdy.

Not his role model.

Not the man who'd vowed he'd remain single for life.

Gabe sent Rowdy a disgusted look. "I guess I *should* have called first."

"You mean you came alone?"

"Hell, yeah," Gabe said. "Why?"

"Just wondering," Rowdy said, grinning at him. "I thought you might have brought the new Mrs. Coulter along."

"And how'd you hear about her?"

"How do you think?"

"Then I'm sure Smitty also told you we only got married for the boy's sake."

"Yeah, Smitty mentioned something like that when I called last week," Rowdy said. "But when he rattled on about how great she was, I figured even an old saddle tramp like you would have enough sense to realize you'd lucked into a pretty good thing."

Gabe took a playful swing at Rowdy.

Rowdy was quick enough to dodge it.

"I hate to say this, Gabe," he teased, "but you look like hell warmed over. And you definitely look like a man who could use a stiff drink."

"You mean *sugar* still lets you drink?" Gabe jeered.

It was Rowdy's turn to take a swing.

They finally settled themselves at Rowdy's

kitchen table with a bottle of bourbon between them. Gabe glanced at the man who was only a year older, thinking how people had often mistaken them for brothers. They were practically the same height and build and, like most cowboys whose time was spent on the open range, Rowdy's blond hair was in bad need of a good haircut.

"So, tell me," Rowdy said after he'd poured them both a second drink. "How bad do you have it for this woman you only married for your nephew's sake?"

Gabe picked up his glass and belted down the liquid. "Let's just say I kissed her over twenty-four hours ago and even this whiskey can't wash away the taste of her lipstick."

Rowdy let out a low whistle. "That bad, huh?"

"That bad."

"Then what in the hell are you doing in Montana, man?"

"I thought if I spent a few days in Montana with you, it might clear my head."

"And what if she's gone when you get back?"

Fear gripped Gabe's heart. The thought of Sara leaving while he was gone had never crossed his mind. Why wouldn't Sara leave? Instead of telling her exactly how he felt, he'd stormed off like the coward that he was. And he'd left her to believe he'd only kissed her to make Ronnie jealous.

"So, what's got you in such a stew, Gabe?" Rowdy leaned forward and filled his glass again. "Does it bother you that Billy's the one who met her first?"

"Hell, no," Gabe said, and he meant it. "She was an innocent kid when she ran into Billy. And we both know my brother never had any scruples when it came to women. Sara never had a chance from the minute Billy said hello."

"So, what's the problem? Is she butt ugly? Hard to get along with? Dumb as a fence post?"

"No, dammit," Gabe said. "She's beautiful. And she's smart and easygoing. Sara is everything a man could want."

"I see. So this isn't about Sara. It's about you. You fooled around and fell in love. And to put it bluntly, you're one scared-shitless cowpoke."

Gabe nodded.

"Exactly what part scares you?"

"Exactly what part doesn't?" Gabe grumbled.

Rowdy snorted. "Hell, Gabe, I don't know about you, but I'm tired of not having anything to keep me warm at night but my own imagination. We've both worked hard. We've both paid our dues. And because of it, we've become successful ranchers. But there comes a time in every man's life when he has to face the fact that being a lone desperado isn't all it's cracked up to be."

Rowdy tilted his head toward his bedroom. “If I’m lucky, that little gal in there is going to marry me. And if you have any sense left in that thick skull of yours, you’ll head back to Colorado. If you don’t, you’ll be getting a divorce before you even find out if you like being married.”

When Gabe refused to comment, Rowdy leaned back in his chair and crossed his arms over his bare chest. “The way I see it, Gabe, it’s the easiest thing in the world to isolate yourself from life and stay hidden out on the range with a bunch of horses who don’t demand a thing but a place to graze and a cool stream to take a drink. But it takes real guts to make a permanent commitment to another human being. I’ve finally grown up. What about you?”

Gabe didn’t answer right away.

But he finally said, “Maybe I’ve grown up, too, Rowdy. As hard as I try, I can’t picture the rest of my life without Sara in it.”

When Rowdy grinned, Gabe said, “At least pacify me with one last toast to those die-hard desperados we both used to be.”

Grabbing the bottle from the middle of the table, Rowdy poured each of them another drink. “To all the young desperados out riding the open range,” he said, clinking his glass against Gabe’s. “And to all the old desperados like us who have finally found their way home.”

"I NEED TWO COOKIES, Mom," Ben announced late Monday afternoon as he raced into the kitchen. "One for me, and one for Bandit."

Sara walked to the cookie jar and handed her son a cookie for each fist, then steeled herself for the loud bang as the screen door slammed behind him. She walked back to the stove, pierced her pot roast several times with a meat fork, then closed the oven door and set the timer. She heard the screen door open again.

"No more cookies, Ben, and I mean it," she called over her shoulder. "You'll ruin your supper." Expecting a lengthy argument, Sara turned around.

The meat fork fell from her hand.

"I thought you were in Montana."

"And I thought you'd be gone when I got back."

Sara blinked rapidly to clear her eyes. "Is that what you want, Gabe? For me to leave?"

"God, no."

He closed the distance between them so fast Sara gasped when he pulled her into his arms. And the searing kiss he gave her left Sara's fingers tangled in the long curls at the nape of Gabe's neck. When they finally broke apart, all they could do was stare at each other.

"I love you, Sara," Gabe said, his gaze searching her face. "I wouldn't blame you if you walked out and never looked back. But I'm asking you to stay and let me prove it to you."

He took her breath away. There was so much she wanted to say the words backed up against the lump in her throat. Finally she managed to say, "I love you, too, Gabe."

He looked surprised. "You do?"

"Completely."

Now that she could speak it was time to put all her cards on the table. "My love comes with only one condition, Gabe. It has to be me. Only me. I won't share you with anyone else."

The lines of his face softened as he met her gaze. "There isn't anyone else, Sara. I've wanted to tell you that from the beginning. But I was afraid—"

Sara touched his lips with her fingertips.

"Don't," she said. "I can't change my past with Billy. And you can't change your past with Ronnie. All I care about is now. And the future I hope we have together."

"There'll never be anyone but you," Gabe promised.

He took her hand, walking backward as he led her in the direction of the stairs. When Sara cast a worried glance at the door, Gabe sent her a guilty look. "There isn't anyone to worry about," he said. "I just sent Smitty into town. He took Ben with him."

"You were pretty sure of yourself, weren't you?" Sara accused, but she didn't halt their progress.

"I was sure I couldn't stand another minute without showing you how much I love you."

"Good answer," Sara said.

He drew her into his arms again when they reached the top of the stairs. He kissed her. Longer this time. And with much more urgency. They more or less stumbled through the door and into Gabe's bedroom.

She could feel the extent of his need, the hardness pressing against her, and the pressure of his firm body close against hers left Sara's mind spinning.

"You are so beautiful," he said as his fingers tackled the buttons of her loose cotton dress.

Sara returned the favor and unbuttoned his shirt.

Within seconds, they were both naked.

She should have felt self-conscious standing stark naked in front of Gabe for the first time in broad daylight. But she didn't. Not with Gabe looking at her the way he was now, his eyes filled with love, his face so full of emotion.

He cupped her face in his hands and he kissed her again. Then he reached up and removed the clip from her hair.

Her hair came loose and tumbled down her back.

Gabe let the long strands slide through his fingers.

"I've wanted to do that forever," he said.

"I'll wear my hair down more often," Sara promised.

"No," he said. "No one sees your hair down but me."

He swept her up then and carried her across the room. When he placed her on his bed, Gabe pulled her close and whispered against her ear, "I want to make love to you, Sara. As my wife. The only woman I want in my life."

Instinctively, he'd known she needed to hear that.

And it only made Sara love Gabe more.

He took his time. Never hurrying, his eyes never leaving her face as his hands roamed slowly over her body. Sara tingled each time he touched her bare skin. And she knew each caress was a pure act of love. He was savoring the moment and allowing her to do the same. Making their first time together special. Sacred. Something they would always remember.

"I want to kiss you here," he said.

His mouth moved to the sensitive hollow of her neck.

Sara closed her eyes and gave in to the sensation.

"And here." His lips moved down to her hardened nipples.

Sara's fingers tangled in his hair.

His tongue moved lower, trailing down her stomach.

"I want to kiss you all over," he whispered.

Slowly, he parted her legs.

Sara's nails dug into his hard bare shoulders.

She whispered Gabe's name when his mouth moved lower.

ONLY AFTER GABE FELT Sara give in to pleasure, did he slide his body up the full length of hers. He paused for a moment, propped up on one elbow, looking down at the woman he loved with all his heart.

He'd never seen anything more beautiful.

Her long hair fanned out across his pillow, and the sight of her flushed cheeks and her swollen lips drove him crazy. Still, he was determined to pleasure her again before he took any pleasure himself. He wanted to take his time, show Sara exactly what it meant for a man to truly love a woman.

She didn't give him that chance.

She pulled his head down for a long kiss.

And then another.

Her hand trailed down his stomach.

Her fingers closed tightly around him.

"Make love to me, Gabe. Now."

Gabe lost all reason.

His hands slid beneath her hips, pulling Sara to

him. There was no holding back now. Nothing to keep them from being swept up in a frenzy of pure driving need.

They both cried out when he slid deep inside her.

Her arms went around his neck. Her legs wrapped around his waist. And Sara became everything. Everything Gabe wanted. All he'd ever need.

Gabe quickly reversed their positions.

He wanted her on top. Wanted Sara to feel him deep inside her. Wanted to heighten her pleasure as they rode one glorious wave of ecstasy after another.

She was getting close.

He could feel it.

He could feel her heat. Her wetness. Her muscles tightening around him as he held on to her hips. He thrust deeper. Moved faster. His own desire mounted as he pushed Sara closer and closer to the point of no return.

Finally, she cried out and collapsed against him.

Her long hair brushed across his face.

And Gabe lost all control.

Breathless, they clung to each other.

Amazed over what they'd just shared.

Aware this was only the beginning.

"I HOPE YOU REALIZE I don't intend to spend another night without you," Gabe said, kissing the top of Sara's head.

Sara snuggled closer to him. "I could be persuaded to pay you a visit after Ben is asleep tonight."

He tilted her chin up to look at him. Sara worried he didn't understand.

"You're right. Ben needs to get used to us as a couple before you move into my bedroom."

Sara kissed him.

Gabe grinned. "What was that for?"

"For always thinking about Ben."

"I'm not thinking about Ben right now," he teased, and reached for her again.

But the unmistakable sound of the flatbed truck pulling into the driveway forced them back to the real world.

Gabe left the bed and began pulling on his jeans. "I'll shower at the bunkhouse," he said. "But I'll buy you some time by stalling Ben and Smitty."

Once dressed, he started for the door.

"Don't say anything to Smitty, okay?"

He paused and gave her a quizzical look.

"I know Smitty isn't stupid," Sara said, "but he'll need time to adjust to us being a couple, too."

Gabe walked back to the bed and kissed her.

"And what was that for?"

"Because I love you," he said, and slipped out the door.

Thirty minutes later, Sara had showered and

was again busy tending her pot roast when Smitty limped into the kitchen whistling a happy tune. He placed the sack of groceries on the table. Sara thanked him as usual and began unloading the paper sack.

"Why, if I didn't know better," Smitty said with an unmistakable gleam in his eye, "I'd say you look a little flushed this afternoon, missy. You ain't running a fever, are you?"

Sara purposely ignored the old rascal's question.

But Smitty wasn't too far off his mark.

She *was* running a fever—a fever that raged through her body every time she thought about the nights she'd be spending in Gabe's bed. For the first time in her life, Sara had everything she'd ever wanted.

Only one pesky thought nagged at the back of Sara's mind: *How can a life so wonderful possibly last for someone like me?*

CHAPTER SEVENTEEN

"I STILL CAN'T BELIEVE next week is Thanksgiving," Betsy commented as she and Sara stood in the back of the kindergarten classroom.

They were watching while Junior and Ben led Joe and Gabe around the room, pointing out pictures of the Pilgrims and turkeys the boys had painted for the holiday open house. This was what the holiday was all about—family, friends, tradition—and for the first time in her life, Sara would celebrate in that fashion. These experiences were like her fantasies. She was overwhelmed. Gratitude laced with fear that none of it would last dogged her.

"Hey? Are you okay?" Betsy grabbed Sara's arm.

She managed a nod.

Betsy fumbled through her purse and quickly produced a rumpled tissue that Sara gladly accepted. She turned her back to compose herself in case Gabe should look up and notice her tears.

"I know you'll think I'm silly," Sara told Betsy,

"but it just crossed my mind that someday Ben will be doing the same thing Gabe is doing now. Walking around with his own son or daughter and telling them all of the things he remembered during his first year of school in this very same room."

Betsy reached out and touched Sara's arm. "I don't think that's silly at all. It's a typical mother's response. Our babies are growing up, and that's not always an easy thing to accept."

"It's more than that for me," Sara said. "By the time I was in second grade, I'd attended four different elementary schools. Thanks to Gabe, Ben will never know that kind of instability."

"Don't you think you should give yourself some credit for Ben's security, Sara? I mean, as grand as Gabe Coulter is, the final decision to bring Ben to Redstone was yours. If Ben has anyone to thank for growing up here, it's you."

Sara smiled. "How do you always know exactly what to say to make me feel better?"

"If I've made you feel better, I'm glad. But we've become close enough friends that I don't intend to let you harbor some ridiculous idea that because you had a rotten childhood you don't have anything to offer your son. Security comes from being loved. Not the ranch. Not the Coulter name. There isn't any substitute for a mother's love, Sara."

As if to confirm Betsy's last statement, Ben called out from across the room, "Hurry, Mom, come look at my desk. I wrote *B-E-N* right here on top all by myself."

"I'm coming." Sara gave Betsy a quick hug before she hurried across the room where Gabe and Ben were currently inspecting the small desk that did indeed have *B-E-N* written in squiggly letters on a piece of construction paper taped to the desktop.

"See, Mom. I can write my own name."

Gabe slid his arm around her shoulder.

"Great job, Ben," Sara said. "Your letters are perfect."

Ben beamed with pride and hurried after Junior.

Gabe pulled her closer. "Am I mistaken? Or were you getting misty-eyed back there?"

"Just a little," Sara admitted.

It always amazed her at how attuned to her Gabe was, as she was to him.

Over the past few months they'd opened up to each other, filled in the blanks of their lives, so different, yet surprisingly so similar. Both of them had been hurt—her never having any family support, Gabe losing the family support he'd always counted on.

She'd told Gabe how being disappointed time after time by a mother who couldn't stay out of trouble had made it difficult for her to trust anyone. And how being passed from one family to another had made her reluctant to get attached to any of the foster families, knowing her stay was only temporary.

She'd also told Gabe she'd gone to a maternity group home after her last foster parents had thrown her out. That she'd been able to graduate high school through a program the home offered. And that although adoption was strongly encouraged, once she'd made it clear she had no intention of giving up her child, the counselors at the home had helped her receive the government assistance she needed until she could find a job and take care of herself and Ben.

Gabe had made his confessions, too.

He'd told her how devastated he'd been when his parents were killed. And he'd told her that losing Billy was the type of pain he wasn't sure he could survive again. He also admitted he'd often blamed himself for Billy's death—for not insisting that Billy stay on the ranch, even though he knew no one could have talked Billy out of following his rodeo-fame dreams.

Sara knew how hard it had been for Gabe to share any of those feelings with her. He was kind and affectionate, but he wasn't the type of man who easily confessed what was on his mind and in his heart.

She'd mentioned that fact to Betsy once.

"Cowboys are a different breed, Sara," Betsy had said. "Their actions speak louder than their words. But you can always count on one thing. Gabe Coulter is cowboy true to the bone."

Cowboy true.

The expression described Gabe to a T.

Loyalty came first with Gabe.

Ironically, although Sara admired that trait, it was Gabe's loyalty that often fueled her own self-doubts. She didn't want her relationship with Gabe based strictly on that level of obligation. She wanted their relationship based on love. And that's why Sara found herself clinging to Betsy's other statement that *actions speak louder than words.*

Over the summer, Gabe had surprised her more than once by sneaking back to the house for a secret lovemaking session. And there had been those long, moonlit walks they'd taken after Ben and Smitty were sound asleep—more proof that what Gabe felt for her went beyond loyalty.

The stolen moments they'd shared beneath the shadows of the big spruce pines surrounding the ranch were some of Sara's fondest memories. And there were other precious memories she'd never forget. Sunday cookouts with the Grahams, Ben and Junior laughing and running across the pasture, Bess, Bandit and Charcoal yapping at their heels. And the horseback rides she'd taken with Ben and Gabe over the ranch, riding the gentle mare Gabe had bought for her.

She'd even acquired a pair of jeans.

And, of course, there were times like tonight.

Having Gabe by her side at Ben's kindergarten open house gave Sara a sense of completeness no words could fully describe. It also reaffirmed her growing belief that the three of them really could make it together as a family.

"Can we stop by Junior's house for dessert before we go home, Mom?" Ben pleaded as he ran up beside them.

As usual, Junior was following close behind.

"We're having punkin pie and ice cream," Junior announced proudly.

When Sara looked to Gabe for an answer, Gabe whispered in her ear, "That's not exactly the type of dessert I had in mind for tonight."

Sara smacked Gabe on the arm.

"Well, can we, Mom?" Ben urged, tugging on the skirt of Sara's dress to get her attention again.

"Of course we can, sweetie," Sara answered. "Go tell Betsy we'll be happy to stop by."

"Traitor," Gabe teased the minute the boys ran off to tell Betsy the good news.

"You shouldn't be naughty in front of the children, Gabe."

"Does that mean can I be naughty when the children aren't around?"

Sara elbowed him this time.

They both sobered when Ben's kindergarten teacher approached. Mrs. Grayson offered a wrinkled smile and said, "I guess you've seen how creative Ben can be with his Thanksgiving drawings."

Gabe and Sara both laughed.

Gabe said, "If you mean the cowboy hats Ben put on his Pilgrims, then yes, we've seen how creative he is."

Sara smiled and said, "And don't forget the Crested-C logo Ben put on the Pilgrims' white bibs."

Mrs. Grayson looked directly at Gabe. "I remember another little Coulter boy who had a fascination with the Crested-C logo when he was in my kindergarten class. And if I remember correctly, that same little boy received a good paddling from me for carving the logo on one of my desks with his pocketknife."

Sara glanced at Gabe in time to see him blush.

"I'd really appreciate you not mentioning that story to Ben, Mrs. Grayson."

"Oh, I bet you would, Gabriel Coulter," the old woman said with a mischievous smile.

She nodded politely to Sara then strolled away.

Sara looked at Gabe and said, "Don't you find

it funny that we were just talking about you being naughty before Mrs. Grayson walked up and confirmed how naughty you've always been?"

Gabe said, "What I find funny is that my kindergarten teacher rescued you from trying to explain why you preferred punkin pie and ice cream to the type of dessert I had in mind."

Sara laughed and linked her arm through Gabe's. "Don't worry, you'll get the kind of dessert you have in mind soon enough."

"Not soon enough for my liking," Gabe complained.

Sara giggled and pulled him toward Ben and the Grahams, who were now waiting for them by the classroom door.

GABE GLANCED in his rearview mirror. The excitement of the open house and too much pie and ice cream had worn Ben out. He was fast asleep. When he glanced at Sara sitting on the seat beside him, Gabe smiled.

Sara smiled back and reached for his hand.

Gabe knew without a doubt that he loved this woman and his nephew more than he ever thought possible. Both Ben and Sara had brought new meaning into his life.

In fact, he was finally beginning to realize that he hadn't had much of a life before. What he'd had were 15,000 acres of land and a hundred different excuses to isolate himself from the very things every human craved most: love and being loved.

Yes, love *was* a risky business.

But Gabe was thankful he'd taken that risk. They'd bonded as a real family, cementing relationships Gabe hoped would last a lifetime. And a lifetime with Ben and Sara was all Gabe wanted. He'd never wanted anything more.

As they started up the steep incline to the ranch, it crossed Gabe's mind that neither he nor Sara had said a word since they left the Graham house. And that was what total contentment meant in his book—being so comfortable with someone you never had to say a word.

He squeezed Sara's hand.

She squeezed back.

Only one thing bothered Gabe. Sara still hadn't moved her things into his bedroom. He suspected she was waiting until their six-month trial period was officially over. He hadn't pushed her to give up her own bedroom. He'd held back, giving her time to make that decision on her own.

But it didn't keep him from worrying.

Having his own family had shown him what the love of a good woman and a child could bring into a man's life. Gabe didn't want to lose that.

And with that thought in mind, Gabe said, "I

was only teasing earlier, you know. As crazy as I am about that sexy body of yours you mean far more to me than just nightly dessert."

Sara sent him an impish grin. "What's the problem, cowboy? Is that your way of trying to back out of dessert tonight?"

"Oh, I'm ready for dessert," Gabe said, sending her a sultry look. "You can count on that."

"Can I have more dessert, too, Mom?" a groggy voice called out from the backseat.

Gabe and Sara both laughed.

But the meaningful look they exchanged said it all.

CHAPTER EIGHTEEN

"IF I EAT another bite," Gabe said, "I'll never be able to get out of this chair."

Sara smiled when Gabe pushed himself back from the dining room table with a loud groan. He'd accused her lately of trying to fatten him up. But as hard as Gabe worked on the ranch, Sara knew it would take more than her Thanksgiving turkey to put even a pound on his rock-hard frame.

The rest of the men gathered around the dining room table never took their eyes from their plates.

"Not me," Smitty said. "I could use one more piece of that pecan pie, missy."

Sara gladly passed the pie in Smitty's direction. Watching these men enjoy the first Thanksgiving meal she'd prepared for her new family meant more to Sara than any of them realized.

"And I want more chocolate-affair cake, Mom," Ben announced, causing all seven men to laugh.

"It's chocolate *éclair* cake, Ben," Sara corrected, but she didn't miss the fixed stare Gabe was sending her.

It constantly amazed her that something as innocent as a slip of the tongue had the power to send shock waves vibrating through both of them. In fact, the intensity of their passion almost scared Sara sometimes. When their eyes locked again, Sara thought she could actually feel the heat pass between them.

But their silent communication also reminded her she was running out of excuses about moving into Gabe's bedroom permanently.

Ben and Smitty had long since gotten used to them as a couple. She and Gabe were openly affectionate with each other in front of both of them. Still, something held her back. And try as she may, Sara couldn't put a finger on it.

"What's really wrong, Sara?" Gabe had asked her point-blank when she'd moved to go to her own bedroom last night.

She hadn't missed the hurt in his eyes. And she knew he hadn't liked her answer when she told him she wasn't sure, only that she needed more time. He'd agreed, but she was well aware that Gabe's patience was beginning to wearing thin.

She chewed absently at her bottom lip as she passed another pie to one of the ranch hands.

At first she'd told herself she was only holding back because their six months weren't officially over. But this was the end of November, and as Gabe had reminded her last night, there were only a few days left until the six-month deadline lapsed.

Maybe after Christmas she would finally let herself believe she and Gabe had a real marriage and would stay together forever. Maybe putting an end to this year and starting a brand-new one would make her feel better about moving her things into his bedroom on a permanent basis.

Maybe then she'd feel as if she really belonged.

"No, it was Sara's marble pound cake, not the chocolate éclair cake, that won her first prize at the county fair," Smitty argued, snapping Sara back to the conversation going on around the table.

"I like her sticky buns best," one of the hands said.

Sticky buns.

Sara looked up. Gabe had one eyebrow arched.

"Maybe Sara should open her own bakery," Slim mentioned, sending Sara a shy look. "Redstone's never had a bakery before."

Sara laughed. "Well, thanks for the vote of confidence, Slim, but like everyone else around here, I'm too busy to take on an outside job."

"Ain't that the truth," Smitty agreed. He turned to Gabe and said, "Speaking of being busy, do you still want me to deliver those two horses to Denver tomorrow?"

Gabe nodded. "And I'll need you to pick up a few pieces of equipment I've ordered, too. Take the flatbed truck to pull the horse trailer. And take someone with you to help load the equipment."

"Guess that means we'll be staying overnight, then," Smitty said. "You know I don't like driving these roads after dark once the snow starts."

"Ben and I are going to be gone tomorrow, too," Sara reminded Gabe. "I told Betsy I'd drive to Grand Junction."

"Yeah, Uncle Gabe," Ben said. "Santa's coming to the mall to see me and Junior. And Junior's gonna pull his beard to see if it's fake."

Everyone at the table laughed.

A few minutes passed before Gabe looked at Sara and said, "Maybe you and Betsy should think about spending the night in Grand Junction and starting back on Saturday, too. Smitty's right. It isn't safe driving these roads with so much snow on the ground."

Sara's heart instantly went out to Gabe. She knew exactly what he was thinking.

"I'll call Betsy as soon as I clear the table," Sara promised. "I'm sure she'd love to spend the night in Grand Junction. That will give us more time to do our Christmas shopping."

"Wow!" Ben chimed in. "Do me and Junior get our own room, Mom?"

"Junior and I," Sara corrected. "And no. We can all stay in one room together."

"Cool," Ben said. "Motels are fun."

Sara looked back at Gabe.

Motel had turned up the heat one more notch.

THE MORNING AFTER Thanksgiving Sara sent a wary look toward the black Suburban parked in front of Jones Country Store where she needed to stop for gas. The menacing Miss Kincaid, however, didn't appear to be anywhere in sight.

They'd crossed each other's paths several times since Founder's Day, but, other than a few mean looks, Ronnie had kept her distance. Still, Sara suspected that a face-to-face showdown between them was inevitable at some point.

Gabe had, after all, chosen her. No woman took that kind of rejection lightly.

"Maybe we should get gas farther down the road," Betsy said, following Sara's gaze to the Suburban.

"No," Sara said, pulling the Cherokee up to the pumps. "I don't intend to spend the rest of my life trying to avoid her. If she still has a problem with Gabe's decision to marry me, it's her problem, not mine."

"You go, girl," Betsy said, but she nodded

toward the backseat. "Still, I think the boys and I should wait in the Jeep. Just to be on the safe side."

"Not a bad idea," Sara agreed, glancing in the backseat. To her relief, Ben and Junior both seemed to be unaware of anything except the two Game Boys that had their full attention.

Sara pumped her gas without incident.

When she headed into the store to pay, Hank Jones looked up from the newspaper he had spread on the counter and greeted her with a wide smile. "I heard you and Betsy were going to Grand Junction for a little Christmas shopping," the old man said when Sara stopped in front of the counter. "And it's a good thing you're getting an early start." He looked down at his watch. "You'll be in Grand Junction by the time the mall opens and before the crowds get heavy."

It amazed Sara at how even the most trivial information seemed to be big news in Redstone.

"I wouldn't have even considered going to the mall the day after Thanksgiving if Santa wasn't making his big appearance. But the boys wore us down."

"Good thing you've decided to stay over tonight, too," Hank said. Sara sent him a surprised look so he added, "Smitty was in here earlier. Said Gabe told you to come back tomorrow. After what happened to Luke and Mary, Gabe has good reason to worry about you and the boy driving up that road with so much snow on the ground."

Sara forced a smile, but she made a mental note to speak to Smitty about being more discreet with the personal details of their lives. Though Sara doubted it would do any good. She accepted her change with a quick nod and hurried for the door before the man had an opportunity to pry even further.

"You be careful, now," Hank called out after her. "And watch out for those crazy drivers in Grand Junction. They'll run you right off the road if you let them."

"Thanks for the warning. And tell Marge I said Happy Holidays."

The second Sara slid behind the wheel of the Cherokee, Betsy said, "Well?"

Sara shook her head. "No problem. Hank was the only one in the store."

After they pulled away, Betsy said, "I was just thinking. If you're getting brave enough to take Ronnie on, it must mean things are going pretty well with you and Gabe."

"Please don't jinx me, Betsy. I'm so happy sometimes I pinch myself to make sure I'm not dreaming."

Betsy raised an eyebrow. "Does that mean what I think it means?"

"No. I haven't moved my things yet."

"But Sara, that's just plain silly," Betsy said. "What's the problem?"

"I swear, Betsy, I don't know."

"Well, if limiting your husband to a quickie every night doesn't suck the romance right out of a relationship, I don't know what will."

Sara sent a nervous look in her rearview mirror. The games still had the boys' full attention.

"I know I'm pushing Gabe to the limit, Betsy. And I know he isn't happy about it. But—"

"You know what your problem is?" As usual, Betsy answered her own question. "You and Gabe have never had the luxury of being completely alone with no one else to worry about. You said yourself you always have one ear open listening for either Ben or Smitty."

"True," Sara agreed. If it wasn't Ben needing one more glass of water, it was Smitty banging around in the kitchen late at night for some warm milk for his insomnia.

"And that's what you and Gabe need. One night alone together. No interruptions."

"And you know that isn't possible."

"But didn't you say Smitty was spending the night in Denver tonight?"

"Yes," Sara said, "and we're spending the night in Grand Junction, remember?"

Betsy grinned. "How are you at power shopping?"

"Excuse me?"

"I say we take the boys to see Santa. We power shop our heads off. Then we head right back to Redstone. You can't miss this opportunity, Sara. Who knows how long it will be before Smitty is out of town again."

"And what about Ben?"

Betsy turned in her seat. "Hey, guys," she said. "Instead of staying in Grand Junction tonight, how would you like it if we come back home after you see Santa and Ben stays with us for a sleepover?"

"Wow. Can I, Mom?" Ben asked. "I've never been to a sleepover before."

"Please, Miss Sara," Junior chimed in.

Sara looked over at Betsy. "Are you sure you wouldn't mind?"

"Oh, pooh," Betsy said. "I insist."

The boys gave each other a high-five.

Betsy leaned toward Sara and whispered, "By the time Ben and Smitty get home tomorrow, I guarantee you and Gabe will be sharing the same closet."

Sara blushed.

"Speed up, girlfriend. We've got to get you back to the Crested-C in time to give Gabe an early Christmas present."

CHAPTER NINETEEN

SARA CHECKED the oven one last time and glanced at her watch. She had thirty minutes to make herself presentable before Gabe and the boys returned from the northern border of the ranch. She knew they'd intended to spend the day checking for damage the heavy snowfall might have done to the fences.

By dusk, they'd be back.

Thankfully, everything was ready and waiting for Gabe to arrive. Her crown roast—Gabe's favorite—was almost done. The champagne was chilling. And since she had already intended to stay in Grand Junction overnight, she'd loaded down the bunkhouse refrigerator the night before with enough Thanksgiving leftovers to last a full week.

That meant the ranch hands would all go straight to the bunkhouse when they returned. And Gabe would find more than a cold turkey sandwich waiting for him when he walked through the door.

Sara smiled, thinking how surprised Gabe would be. She'd even thought to park the Cherokee at the back of the house so Gabe wouldn't see it from the barn. He'd come through the door thinking he was entering an empty house. And what he'd find instead was her, dressed in the skimpy little black dress she'd bought in Grand Junction.

Walking into the dining room, Sara checked the table one last time, pleased with her candlelit dinner-for-two preparations. She reached out and rearranged the bottle of champagne, then ran her fingers over the delicate roses etched into the ornate silver ice bucket that had belonged to Gabe's mother.

"Roses were Mary's favorite," Smitty had told her once, making Sara think of the framed wedding portrait of Luke and Mary in Gabe's office. Before she headed upstairs, Sara went to look at their picture.

How young and full of hope they both seemed. Luke tall and proud. Mary beaming from the knowledge that the man she married had stood before God and everyone else and pledged his life to her alone.

According to Smitty, the whole town had attended the ceremony. He'd told Sara about the wedding during one of the chats that had become their morning routine when he came in for his grocery list.

"Biggest wedding ever to hit Redstone," he'd said. "Luke and Mary were married out on the front lawn." He'd reminisced about how Mary had ridden up the long driveway in a horse-drawn carriage decorated with pink and white roses. "Everyone said Mary was the most beautiful bride they ever saw. And that's a fact."

Stepping closer to the portrait, Sara couldn't help but admire the Victorian-style wedding dress Mary had made herself. The dress was carefully stored in a cedar chest in Sara's room. She would have loved to have worn that dress the day she married Gabe.

But there was no point in idle wishes.

Nor did it serve any purpose dreaming of things that weren't meant to be. Better instead to focus on what she could have—an intimate dinner alone with the man she loved completely, followed by an entire night of blissful and totally uninterrupted lovemaking.

Untying her apron, Sara walked out of Gabe's office and right into her worst enemy.

"What are you doing here?"

Ronnie's mocking smile was lethal. "I was about to ask you the same thing. I thought you were staying in Grand Junction tonight."

Panic seized Sara for a moment.

But reason calmed her back down. "Are you implying Gabe invited you here?"

"Are you stupid enough to believe that he didn't?"

It was on the tip of Sara's tongue to tell Ronnie to leave. To get out of her house and never come back. She tried, but Sara couldn't spit the words out. And the longer she stared at Ronnie, the more clear it became why she couldn't. This wasn't her house. It was Gabe's house. And it would never be her house as long as she settled for being Gabe's afterthought wife.

"I am stupid enough to believe Gabe didn't invite you here, Ronnie. I just didn't realize how stupid I've been about everything else."

Sara took a step forward.

Ronnie took two steps back.

"If you're smart you'll leave before Gabe gets home," Sara told her. She shoved her apron into Ronnie's midsection, pushed past Ronnie and headed for the kitchen.

"And if you're smart you'll stay gone!" Ronnie yelled.

Sara never looked back.

She grabbed her coat and purse from the coatrack. She lifted the keys to the Cherokee from the rack. She slammed the kitchen door behind her. But she didn't let herself cry until she reached the gateposts marking the entrance to the Crested-C Ranch.

Turning off the ignition, Sara sat there for almost thirty minutes, tears streaming down her cheeks. She knew what she had to do. And she knew the big risk she'd be taking if she found the courage to do it. *How am I ever going to explain to Ben if we have to leave?*

Before her heart betrayed her, Sara turned the ignition, then drove decidedly through the gates of the Crested-C Ranch.

SIX MONTHS EARLIER Ronnie would have been thrilled that Sara stormed off the Crested-C because of her. But now, Ronnie found Sara's leaving a hollow victory at best.

And that's what she got for listening to town gossip.

And for letting her pride get the better of her.

Damn Hank Jones! Ronnie fumed.

The old fart had purposely needled her in front of a store full of customers. Throwing it in her face that Gabe was so in love with his new wife he'd told her to stay in Grand Junction rather than risk her driving icy roads at night. Yet, as Ronnie walked into the dining room, she couldn't for the life of her understand why Hank's teasing had made her so angry earlier.

She hadn't even thought about Gabe in months. She'd been too busy.

Busy with her own life—and with Charlie.

Thinking about Charlie struck a chord of fear

deep inside Ronnie's soul. What if he didn't believe that she never would have shown up if she'd known Sara was home? Or that the only reason she'd even stopped by the Crested-C was to rattle Gabe's chain a little—to pay him back for…

Ronnie swallowed.

Pay him back for what? would be Charlie's first question. Funny, but she didn't even have an answer. Not anymore. Not after months of lying in Charlie's arms every night and experiencing for the first time what it truly meant to be loved by a man.

She'd acted on a stupid whim.

And now she was in deep shit.

With Gabe. But more importantly, with Charlie.

Ronnie grabbed the champagne bottle from the ice bucket. She didn't even flinch when the cork made a loud pop. She reached for a glass from the table and filled it all the way to the brim. But she couldn't keep her hand from shaking slightly as she brought the glass to her suddenly parched lips.

In typical hell-bent fashion, she'd screwed up. Only this time, she had everything to lose.

All because of blind ambition that made no sense whatsoever when she thought about it. Merging their two ranches had been a ridiculous idea from the start. Gabe would never leave the Crested-C any more than she would move off her land. The Flying-K meant everything to her. It was where she was born and the Flying-K was where she intended to die.

Gabe had never been the right man for her.

She needed a drifter like Charlie.

A man with no ties to pull him anywhere else.

Pouring another glass of champagne, Ronnie took a long sip as she carefully weighed her options. She could stay and apologize—definitely not her strong point. Or she could leave before Gabe got home and tell Charlie Sara simply got the wrong idea when she stopped by.

So? Why in the hell did you stop by? would be Charlie's next question. And that brought her right back to where she started. There simply wasn't any excuse that would ever be good enough to justify what she'd done.

Ronnie poured her third glass of champagne.

She might as well get drunk.

Drunk was the only state in which she could even imagine apologizing to Gabe.

"LOOKS LIKE you've got company, boss," Slim said as they topped the ridge overlooking the house.

Gabe swore at the sight of the black Suburban. He nudged his spurs into Bruiser's sides, forcing the big steed into a full gallop. A few minutes later he pulled Bruiser to a stop with a quick jerk of the reins, Slim on his horse right beside them.

Gabe hopped off Bruiser, tossed Slim the reins and headed for the kitchen door.

He'd allowed himself to believe Ronnie had given up on her threat to cause him trouble. But now Gabe cursed himself for being that dense. If Sara found out Ronnie had shown up on their doorstep…

Gabe stormed into the kitchen and wasted no time yelling Ronnie's name.

"In here."

He found her sitting at his dining room table, pouring champagne into one of his mother's long-stemmed crystal glasses. She smiled and held her glass up in a toast.

"What in the hell are you doing here?"

Her smile instantly evaporated.

Gabe glanced around the dining room for the first time. The elaborately set table had Sara's name written all over it. Two place settings. The candles. The champagne Ronnie was drinking.

He took a threatening step in her direction. "What have you done, Ronnie? Tell me now."

"I haven't done anything," she said, standing to face him. But the fear in her eyes called her a liar.

"Where's Sara?" Gabe demanded. "Answer me, dammit!"

"To hell with Sara!"

She tossed her champagne in Gabe's face, then threw her glass against the wall.

"Can I help it if that silly bitch you married got the wrong impression?" she yelled. "I only came by to ask you a favor. She's the one who stormed out of here, mumbling something about being stupid."

Gabe lost it.

He grabbed Ronnie by the arm so fast she stumbled, losing her balance. He pulled her to her feet, then dragged Ronnie across the dining room and into the kitchen. When they reached the door, Gabe opened the door and pushed Ronnie through it.

"If you ever come near Sara again," Gabe warned, "I won't be responsible for what I do. And that isn't a threat, Ronnie. That's a promise."

"You go straight to hell, Gabe Coulter. Do you hear me? Straight to hell."

Gabe slammed the door in her face.

He'd never been so angry.

Gabe also had the sickening feeling Ronnie wouldn't be the only female giving him those same directions before the night was over.

"YES, SARA'S HERE, Gabe," Betsy said into the phone. "But maybe it would be better if you wait and come over tomorrow." She sent an apologetic look in Sara's direction. "I'm sorry, Sara. He hung up on me. I'm sure that means Gabe is on his way over here now."

"It's okay, Betsy," Sara said with a sigh. "The sooner we get things settled, the better it will be for all of us."

Betsy shook her head sadly. "You're really scaring me. You're much too calm about this whole thing. I can't imagine how I'd be reacting if Ronnie showed up at my house when she thought I wasn't home."

Sara didn't answer. But she was relieved her demeanor was calm and collected on the outside. She'd had a lifetime of hiding her true feelings. She was a master at it. And she needed to appear in control when Gabe arrived.

How funny that a visit from Ronnie Kincaid had finally opened Sara's eyes. Her only hope now was that Gabe would listen to what she had to say and understand why she'd left the ranch instead of asking Ronnie to leave.

"I'll go up and check on the boys and give you and Gabe some privacy," Betsy said when the sound of a vehicle in the Grahams' driveway snapped Sara from her thoughts.

Sara thanked her then headed for the door. She opened it the minute Gabe stepped foot on the porch.

"Are you okay?" Gabe asked.

Sara nodded.

He reached out and pulled her to him in a full

embrace. She refused to sink into him, to let his strength soothe her. Eventually he released her.

"We need to talk."

He let out a long sigh, but he followed her into the living room. Sara took a seat on the sofa, while Gabe remained standing.

He raked a hand through his hair, looking at her with a worried expression on his face. "I can only guess what happened before I got home," he said. "But you have to believe me, Sara. I didn't invite Ronnie to the ranch tonight."

"Give me a little credit, Gabe," Sara told him. "I know you didn't invite Ronnie. I know you wouldn't do that."

He sat beside her, obviously puzzled. "Then I don't understand. If you knew I didn't invite her, why didn't you tell Ronnie to leave?"

Sara prayed he would understand. "I didn't have the right to ask her to leave."

Gabe frowned. "Of course you did. It's your house."

Sara shook her head. "No, Gabe. The house belongs to you and Ben. Just like the ranch belongs to you and Ben. Gabe Coulter and Ben Coulter, the two owners of the Crested-C."

He looked even more confused.

And Sara couldn't blame him.

She knew she was rambling. She kept grasping

for the right words to explain. But sitting this close to Gabe was distracting. She stood and walked away. And when she turned around, Sara crossed her arms, hugging herself tightly as she gathered the courage to say everything she needed to say.

"You know I've been holding back, Gabe. But I honestly didn't know why I wouldn't move into your bedroom permanently until Ronnie walked through the door tonight. The minute I couldn't ask her to leave, I knew. As much as I've tried to convince myself it doesn't matter how we got together, it does. I don't want to spend the rest of my life wondering if you truly love me, or if you just settled for loving me because it was best for Ben."

A muscle twitched in his jaw. "What am I supposed to say to that, Sara? I can't change how we got together. And neither can you."

"Say we can start over," Sara told him.

Hope flashed across his face.

Then Sara said, "Have the marriage annulled like you promised."

The hope was replaced by anger. But Sara knew she couldn't back down now.

"And that's your idea of starting over?" he mocked. "By putting an end to our marriage?"

"Our fake marriage, Gabe," Sara reminded him. "I want the real thing. And if you decide to ask me to marry you again, I want you to ask me for one reason and one reason only. Because you love me. Not to fulfill your obligation to Ben."

He kept staring at her as if she were crazy. She clenched her fists to stop their trembling.

"I'd never take Ben away from Redstone, Gabe," Sara said softly. "I wouldn't do that to Ben or to you. But I think Ben and I should move into town and give you some time to think things over and decide what you really want."

He frowned. "I already know what I want. Do you?"

Sara nodded. "I told you. I want to start over."

"Are you kidding me? You go your way? I'll go mine? And if we happen to meet up again along the way, you'll be satisfied we were meant to be together?" His laugh was bitter. "Why don't you just come out and say what you really mean, Sara? You're not sure you love me."

"That isn't true," Sara protested. "I do love you. I love you with all my heart. But I want it all, Gabe. I want to be wooed first, like any other woman. And when you propose, I want you to do it because you can't live without me. I want a real wedding, not a fake one. I want to wear your mother's wedding dress. I want to ride up the driveway to the Crested-C in a horse-drawn carriage filled with roses. And I want the whole town standing on the front lawn when you tell the world I'm the one you want for the rest of your life."

When he kept staring at her, Sara said, "I'm sorry. I want to be wanted for me, for who I am. I want a real marriage. Not a marriage of convenience."

"A marriage of convenience?" He laughed again. "Don't you have that backward? If anything, this has been a marriage of *inconvenience* for both of us. I wasn't ready for a wife. And you weren't looking for a husband. But somehow through all the insanity we still managed to fall in love. And if that isn't good enough for you, Sara, then I'm the one who's sorry."

He stood, and the look on his face said she'd hurt him deeply.

"I've tried to prove I love you every way I know how. But if you expect me to jump through hoops like some trained poodle, you've picked yourself the wrong damn cowboy."

"Obviously, I have," Sara snipped. She couldn't help it, she didn't like his tone. And she sure didn't care for his superior attitude.

"So?" he said. "Where does that leave us?"

He kept staring at her.

Sara kept holding his gaze.

"If you aren't willing to start over," Sara said, "I guess that leaves me no choice but to move to Redstone."

"Dammit! I didn't say I wasn't willing to start over."

"As long as we start over on your non-poodle terms, you mean?"

"Now you're twisting my words around," he accused.

"Is it really too much to ask, Gabe? Can you really not understand why the relationship we have now isn't going to work for me long-term?"

"Stop beating around the bush, Sara. Is it over between us, or isn't it?"

Sara wasn't ready to give up. "We started out trying to do what was best for Ben, Gabe. All I want is to do what's best for *us* now."

"What's best for all of us is for you to go upstairs and get Ben and come home with me," Gabe shouted.

Lord, that was the one thing she couldn't do.

"No," she said. "I've told you how I feel. If you can't understand that, then Ben and I will move."

She'd never seen him so angry.

Not even at the Founder's Day kissing booth.

"Then you do what you have to do, Sara," he said, his jaw set and rigid. "And I'll start the divorce proceedings. But it isn't fair to spoil Ben's Christmas. At least stay at the ranch until Christmas is over."

It isn't fair to spoil Ben's Christmas.

His words hit Sara with the force of a tidal wave.

She'd gambled that Gabe loved her—and she'd lost.

It had been all about Ben in the beginning.

It was still all about Ben now.

She was standing here, pouring her heart out, and begging him to save their relationship. And all Gabe cared about was not spoiling Ben's Christmas.

But damn if she'd let him see how much he'd hurt her.

"You're right," Sara said, her voice so calm she scared herself. "It isn't fair to spoil Ben's Christmas. We'll stay at the ranch until after Christmas. That should give me enough time to find a place in town."

Gabe walked out of the Grahams' living room.

He never looked back.

CHAPTER TWENTY

THE SHORT DRIVE from the Grahams' house back to the Crested-C was only five miles. But it was the longest trip Gabe had ever made. He arrived home to an empty house, except for the smoke-filled kitchen that greeted him the minute Gabe opened the back door. Gabe waved away the heavy smoke, grabbed an oven mitt from the counter and managed to pull Sara's surprise dinner from the oven.

He threw the burned pan out into the yard.

The same way Sara had thrown away their future.

Holding the kitchen door open wide, Gabe let the smoke clear for a good ten minutes. The frigid Colorado night air didn't even faze him. Sara's words had already left him too numb inside to feel a damn thing.

What a fool he'd been. He'd opened his heart again. And love had brought him right back to his knees.

But he'd never make that mistake again.

Finally closing the door, Gabe turned off the oven and started in the direction of the back stairs. He stopped when he remembered the dining room and the intimate dinner he and Sara should have shared.

The thought should have saddened him.

Instead, it only made Gabe mad as hell.

He spent the next hour in a full-blown fury removing all signs of the private party that would have been a magical night for both of them. And only after everything had been disposed of and put away did Gabe feel that some semblance of order had been restored to his life. He switched off the light the same way he intended to switch off his feelings. He only wished he could dispose of other reminders of Sara as easily.

But the next few weeks were going to be pure hell.

And Gabe knew it.

He'd put on a good front for Ben's sake. But if Sara had any sense, she'd stay out of his way. He'd handed her his love, his heart and everything else he owned on a goddamn silver platter. And tonight she'd thrown it all in his face with the flimsy excuse about wanting it all.

Well, he had news for Sara.

He'd given all he had to give her.

And if that wasn't enough, to hell with her.

He was going get a good night's sleep. And he was going to be out on the open range where he belonged when Sara came back to the ranch tomorrow.

In his bedroom Gabe jerked off his shirt and his thermal undershirt and threw them to the floor. He kicked off his boots, and he pulled off his jeans. But instead of sleeping nude, waiting for Sara to come warm his bed for a few hours, Gabe told himself with certainty that having nothing but his thermal underwear bottoms to keep him warm in the winter would suit him fine.

Hours later as he tossed and turned in bed, however, more serious thoughts began running through his mind. Like maybe it would be better if Sara did move on. Let her find a man willing to ask *How high?* the minute she said *Jump.* That wasn't the kind of marriage he wanted. Marriage was a fifty-fifty deal, dammit. And by God, he'd done his part.

Sara was the one who wouldn't commit.

Rolling over on his side, Gabe punched his fist deep into his pillow, more convinced than ever that he was right and Sara was wrong and that any man willing to go along with her ridiculous demands was a damn idiot. Ben certainly didn't deserve such a roller-coaster ride—married…not married…married again.

Bullshit. That's what it was.

The whole point in bringing them to Colorado

had been to provide some stability in their lives. He thought he'd done that—until tonight.

Gabe rolled onto his back again, staring at the ceiling. Of course, now that he and Sara wouldn't be trying to juggle a romance, at least Ben would be their main focus again. So maybe all hadn't been lost. Ben would still have his mother's love and support. And Gabe would still be here to give Ben the direction any young boy needed.

They'd just do it separately.

"I'm fine with this," Gabe told his empty room.

Liar! the four walls yelled back.

SARA PURPOSELY WAITED until she was sure Gabe had left the ranch before she headed to the Crested-C the following morning. And thanks to Betsy's generous offer, Ben had stayed behind to play with Junior. Betsy would drop Ben off later, giving Sara a little more time to regroup and pull herself together.

She drove up the driveway with a heavy heart. She spied Bandit hovering near the back porch, his head bent over a scorched baking pan lying in the yard.

"My crown roast!" Sara groaned.

In all the confusion, she'd forgotten the oven.

Rattled at the thought of how easily she could have burned down the whole house, Sara jumped out of the Jeep and shooed Bandit away from his findings. She hurried into the house with the seared pan under her arm, relieved to see that other than the stench of stale smoke, everything in the kitchen seemed intact.

She stopped dead still, however, when a trip to the dining room found no remains of her preparations. In an instant, Sara knew it was Gabe's way of telling her he'd wiped the slate clean. He wanted no reminders of what might have been. No telltale signs that the previous night could have been special. His actions had made everything crystal clear. Gabe wasn't willing to give her anything more than he already had.

Sara took a deep breath, then turned her back on the dining room.

The same way Gabe had turned his back on her.

She had just placed the scorched pan into a sink of suds and hot water, when the back door opened and Smitty hobbled in. His grunt matched the sour look on his face.

"Dang-blast it!" he barked in Sara's direction. "I leave this ranch for one stinking day, and the whole damn place goes to hell in a handbasket. What's all this nonsense about you and Ben moving to town after Christmas?"

Sara shot Smitty a warning look. "Don't start with me, Smitty. If you know Ben and I are moving to Redstone after Christmas, then I'm sure Gabe filled you in on the rest of the story."

The old man snorted. "Yeah, Gabe told me his side. Now I'm ready to hear yours."

Sara let out a long sigh as she looked at the old man she had grown to love despite his irritating personality. Sara motioned for him to take a seat at the table then started making coffee. Once she had the brew perking, Sara sat beside him.

"I'm sure my version isn't any different from the one you've already heard from Gabe."

Smitty frowned. "And you're really willing to let some loony tune like Ronnie Kincaid tear your family apart?"

"This isn't about Ronnie," Sara said. "Gabe and I have both been fooling ourselves. We started out trying to do what was best for Ben, and somehow got caught up in the silly notion that our marriage could turn into the real thing."

"You mean the two of you won't let your marriage turn into the real thing," Smitty argued.

Sara shook her head in protest. "No, I mean exactly what I said. Gabe and I were doomed from the beginning. I think it will be best if Ben and I find our own place to live."

"And I think you and Gabe both deserve a hard kick in the backside for letting your own stubbornness destroy this family," Smitty declared.

"And did you inform Gabe of that fact?"

"You bet I did."

"And Gabe's response?" Sara asked hopefully.

"What do you think?" Smitty grumbled. "Gabe told me to mind my own business."

Sara covered his wrinkled hand with hers. "Then I guess there's no reason for me to repeat that suggestion, is there?"

"No," the old man mumbled. "But when it comes to Ben, I intend to make this my business." He sent Sara a pleading look. "Don't you have any idea how much I love that little boy of yours?"

Sara sniffed. "Of course I know how much you love Ben. Just as I know how much Ben loves you and Gabe. And that's why I'd never leave Redstone. Ben needs all of us. There simply isn't any way I can continue living this charade."

"It seemed to be working pretty well, if you ask me."

"Only on the surface, Smitty," Sara said. She rose, filled two cups with coffee, then returned to her seat. "I want what Luke and Mary had," Sara told him. "And if Gabe can't feel that way about me, I need to move on. For his sake and for mine."

A few moments of silence passed between them.

Smitty sent her a disheartened look. "So? Have you given any thought about how you're going to support yourself?"

Was Smitty kidding?

She'd spent her entire life thinking about how she was going to support herself. She'd always been a backup-plan kind of person out of sheer necessity. Just as she'd always known in the back of her mind playing the role of Gabe's wife wouldn't last forever.

Still, how tragic.

It hurt to admit she'd been right all along.

"Well," Sara said, "Betsy mentioned the old Blake house in town was empty. And that the last people who lived there ran a small restaurant in the lower level."

Smitty snorted. "Yeah, and that's why those people aren't there now. Redstone already has two restaurants. Even with the tourist overflow we get from the ski resorts, Redstone isn't big enough to support three full-time restaurants."

"But Redstone doesn't have a bakery."

Smitty looked at her for a moment, then he grinned. "No, Redstone doesn't have a bakery. And that's a fact."

"Does that mean you think a bakery might have a chance of making it in Redstone?"

"The way you bake? I wouldn't be surprised if people came all the way from Aspen for one of your apple turnovers."

Sara laughed. "No one would drive sixty miles for an apple turnover."

"Sure they would," Smitty said, "if they were fresh from the oven."

"Fresh from the oven," Sara repeated slowly.

She leaned over and kissed the old man on the cheek.

Smitty blushed scarlet. "Now why'd you go and do that?"

"For naming my new bakery," Sara told him.

They talked a little longer, with Smitty promising to check around and find out what he could about the Blake house. After he left, Sara took their coffee cups to the sink and dropped them into the soapy water.

Once again, she was starting over.

But as frightening as that thought was, in her heart Sara knew she had no other choice. She had to take the first step toward healing the type of self-doubts that had never allowed her to believe she was worthy of love or happiness. She had to learn to believe in herself—to reach out and embrace happiness knowing she deserved it. Only then would she ever be able to give her love to Gabe or anyone else completely.

It was time to make her own place in Redstone.

No more just passing through.

No more being the outsider.

All of it—or nothing.

That was Sara's new motto.

GABE REMOVED Bruiser's saddle, but he spent more time than usual grooming the big steed. He'd been in a somber mood all day, dying a little inside one minute at the thought of Sara and Ben leaving the ranch, and consoling himself the next minute with the knowledge that things could have been worse.

Sara could have gone back to Texas.

At least he could still be a part of their lives.

He spent a little more time than needed straightening up the tack room before he reluctantly headed for the house. He wasn't looking forward to putting on a brave face for Ben. And he definitely wasn't looking forward to seeing Sara for the first time since their big fight. But if she expected him to walk through the door with a hangdog expression, trying to make her feel sorry for him, she was wrong. He'd told her at the beginning he'd annul the marriage if she wanted out.

A man was only as good as his word.

And his word had never been half-assed.

The minute Gabe opened the kitchen door, Ben bounded out of nowhere and jumped straight into his arms. "Me and Junior saw Santa, Uncle Gabe, and I made sure Santa knew how to find me here at the ranch."

Gabe gave his nephew a big hug. He looked

over the top of Ben's head and forced a smile in Sara's direction. "It sure smells good in here."

A look of relief washed across her face.

Sara had obviously been dreading this moment as much as he had. She mouthed *Thank you,* before saying, "Supper should be on the table in about twenty minutes. You boys have plenty of time to wash up first."

She turned back to the simmering pots on the stove.

Gabe lowered Ben to the floor. "Ready, partner? You can tell me all about Santa while we wash up."

"Junior didn't pull Santa's beard," Ben said as he vaulted up the stairs ahead of Gabe. "He was too scared he wouldn't get any presents."

Gabe laughed and followed Ben to the upstairs bathroom. Their time together in the evenings while they washed up for supper had become a nightly ritual.

Once inside the bathroom, Ben dragged the small stool Smitty had made for him out of the linen closet. He propped himself against the sink while Gabe opened the medicine cabinet and took out his shaving gear.

"Will you and Smitty be moving to town with me and Mom after Christmas, Uncle Gabe?"

An innocent question, but it hit Gabe like a hammer.

"Mom says the road to the ranch gets real retcherous in January, and a big boy like me needs to be in town so I won't miss any school."

So that had been Sara's explanation. She sure hadn't wasted any time telling Ben.

But Gabe knew Sara was only giving Ben plenty of time to adjust. It would make it much easier on Ben when it came time for them to leave.

Gabe squirted a small dab of his shaving cream into Ben's outstretched hand before he said, "Your mother's right. The road to the ranch can be treacherous during January. And big boys like you can't afford to miss any school. But Smitty needs to stay here at the ranch and take care of the livestock. And so do I."

Ben patted his baby cheeks with the white foam before he sent Gabe a concerned look. "You won't give my room to anyone else while I'm gone, will you, Uncle Gabe?"

Another innocent question—straight to the gut.

"No way," Gabe said. "That room belonged to your daddy, and now it belongs to you and no one else."

Gabe picked up his razor and raked it down his cheek.

"But what about Bandit? Can Bandit live with me in town? Or will he have to stay here at the ranch?"

Gabe rinsed off his razor before he said, "Well,

I'm not sure Bandit would enjoy being away from the ranch, Ben. But that doesn't mean he can't go to town for a visit now and then."

"And will you come to town for a visit now and then, Uncle Gabe?" Ben pressed.

The questions were killing him.

"Sure. And on weekends when there isn't any school, I don't see why you can't come here."

Ben's eyes widened. "For a sleepover? Just like at Junior's?"

Gabe reached out and ruffled his nephew's hair. "Just like at Junior's."

Satisfied with his uncle's answer, Ben reached for the old bladeless razor Smitty had given him and went about his own version of shaving. Once they had both rinsed their razors in the sink, Ben looked up at him and said, "I'm really going to miss you, Uncle Gabe."

A searing pain this time, straight to the heart.

Gabe lifted Ben off the stool and waited until Ben returned the stool to the closet before he said, "I'm going to miss you, too, Ben. But sometimes we have to do things we don't like because it's the best thing for us to do."

"Like when Mom makes me eat those green peas I hate?"

Gabe laughed. "I couldn't have put it better myself."

He swung Ben onto his shoulders for their trip to the dining room. And after placing Ben in his chair, Gabe took his own seat at the opposite end of the table from Sara. Everyone automatically bowed their heads for Ben's nightly prayer.

Except Gabe.

He sat rigid in his seat, listening to Ben's small voice echo through the room, and fully aware of how empty life was going to be when Ben and Sara moved to Redstone.

CHAPTER TWENTY-ONE

RONNIE GLANCED at her bedside clock and frowned. It was ten o'clock and Charlie still hadn't come to her. The thought of his hard, naked body on top of hers drove her crazy most of the time. The same way the thought of his hard, naked body on top of hers was driving her crazy right now.

She'd told herself for months that what she felt for Charlie was purely physical, but she'd secretly known it was more than that. It was a million different things, when she thought about it. Charlie could be rough and crude when she was in the mood for rough and crude, or he could hold her so tenderly it almost brought tears to her eyes. And to her, tears were as foreign as ballet lessons.

Charlie accepted her for who she was and didn't try to change her—not that it would have done him any good to try. He loved her. And he told her he loved her often. The big surprise was Ronnie liked being loved.

So where the hell was he?

Ronnie glanced at the clock again. Now it was ten-fifteen. She threw the covers back, left the bed and was dressed in minutes, then started her hunt for her tardy lover. She found Charlie in the bunkhouse playing cards.

He barely glanced in her direction when she stormed in.

"Meet me outside," she ordered.

"I'm busy."

No one at the table said a word.

They knew better.

"Then get *un*busy," Ronnie told him.

Charlie cursed and threw down his cards.

Ronnie marched out of the bunkhouse. She was halfway across the yard when Charlie caught up with her. He grabbed her by the arm and spun her around. "What's your damn problem?"

Ronnie was livid. "Don't you *ever* embarrass me in front of my ranch hands like that again."

He laughed. "You're a fine one to talk about embarrassing somebody. Do you think I haven't heard about the visit you paid Gabe Coulter last night when you didn't think his wife was home? How embarrassed do you think I am right now? Everybody knows I've been sharing your bed."

Ronnie lifted her chin. "Nothing happened."

"Only because Gabe threw your ass out!"

"That's his version," Ronnie yelled. "I wouldn't wipe my feet on Gabe Coulter."

Charlie stuck a finger under her nose. "And you're through wiping your feet on me."

He stomped toward the barn.

Ronnie marched after him.

"What the hell's that supposed to mean?"

Charlie whirled to face her. "Exactly what I said. I'm done, Ronnie. You did what you set out to do. Gabe's wife is leaving him."

Ronnie's mouth dropped open. "I don't believe you."

"Believe it," Charlie said. "Just don't expect me to stick around for Gabe's sloppy seconds. I'm leaving in the morning. And I won't be back."

He marched off again.

"Come back here, dammit!" Ronnie called out as she followed.

If Gabe hadn't acted like such an ass when he stormed into the dining room, she would have apologized as she'd planned. But Gabe had looked at her with such contempt in his eyes that a lifetime of rejection had thrown her into a full-blown rage. She'd lashed out in anger—the only way she knew how.

And now it was costing her everything she wanted.

"Dammit, Charlie. Stop and listen to me for a minute."

Charlie didn't stop until they reached the barn. When he did turn around he grabbed Ronnie by the shoulders and shook her so hard her teeth rattled. "No, you listen to me. Only God knows why I love you, Ronnie. You sure as hell aren't an easy person to love. But I know you. Gabe's free now. And you'll never be able to leave him alone."

"Yes, I will," Ronnie vowed. "I swear it."

Charlie pushed her away.

But Ronnie grabbed his arm. "I want you, Charlie." It was the closest thing to begging Ronnie had ever done when she added, "Please. Tell me. What can I do to convince you of that?"

He jerked his arm free, unimpressed. "Patch things up with Gabe and his wife. Until you do, don't come looking for me."

He spun around and headed to the bunkhouse.

Ronnie stood there, too shocked to move.

Gabe and Sara Coulter both hated her guts and Charlie damn well knew it. He'd picked the one thing he knew she couldn't do. And he'd done so on purpose.

"Screw you, Charlie Biggs!"

The loud bang as Charlie slammed the bunkhouse door only made Ronnie more angry. She stomped across the yard, stormed into the house and slammed her front door even harder.

Let Charlie leave. Good damn riddance!

Gabe's wife might be a twit, but the woman wasn't stupid. She'd make Gabe squirm and threaten to take the kid away from him, but they'd be back together by the end of the week. Then who was going to feel like a first-class fool? That's right. Charlie.

The slam of her bedroom door only fueled Ronnie's fury. She kicked off her boots, ripped off her shirt and wiggled out of her jeans. She threw her right boot at the mirror over her dresser, shattering glass all over her bedroom floor. Her left boot sailed through the air and knocked the picture of her sitting on her first pony off the wall with a loud thud.

Charlie would be back.

She was sure of it.

But when he did come crawling back begging her forgiveness, she had news for Charlie. She'd laugh in his stupid, good-for-nothing face.

CHAPTER TWENTY-TWO

SARA AND BETSY WAITED until the pretty real estate agent in the bright gold blazer unlocked the door to the Blake house and ushered them inside. The blonde, Karen, had driven from Aspen to show them the property. And she'd brought her high-rent-district attitude along with her.

"The lease is fifteen hundred a month," Karen said. "A little steep for a town the size of Redstone, but it's the price you pay for being on the main street."

Sara walked across the sizable front room.

"The kitchen is right through those doors, and there's plenty of living space upstairs."

Sara peered into the spacious kitchen.

"The homey atmosphere should be perfect for a bakery," Karen assured them. "Atmosphere, after all, is what most tourists are looking for when they come to a quaint little town like Redstone. Add a few rustic tables and chairs in here and it'll look perfect."

"The place does have charm," Betsy agreed.

"Yes, it does," Sara said, "but it's been sitting empty well over a year. And even with it being on Redstone Boulevard, it's still on the lower end of town. That makes me doubt the location. I also have to consider the improvements I'd have to make before I could open the bakery. The floors are scarred, the walls need painting, and this is just the downstairs. We haven't even seen the upstairs yet." Sara glanced at Karen.

She forced a smile and said, "But the upstairs isn't something you would have to worry about immediately. You could postpone any improvements you wanted to make until the bakery began showing a profit."

"True," Sara said, "but I still can't justify paying fifteen hundred a month for a place I'll have to fix up. Not when I've already been offered a suitable space for the bakery for only nine fifty closer to the other shops."

"Nine fifty?" Karen repeated, obviously shocked.

Sara nodded.

Karen flipped through her notebook. "You know," she mused, "nine fifty might not be out of the question. You're right about the place standing vacant for so long. And it *is* farther from the rest of the other shops." She tapped a manicured finger against a page. "Why don't I just run out to my car and give the owner a quick call on my cell? Nine fifty might be doable in this situation."

"Sorry," Betsy drolled, "I'm afraid your *cell* is useless in this *quaint* little town. You'll have to use the pay phone at Jones Country Store."

Karen looked perturbed then scurried out the door.

Betsy burst out laughing. "What space are you talking about? I didn't know anything else was for rent on Redstone Boulevard."

Sara sent Betsy a sly smile. "You're forgetting I've been on my own a long time, Betsy. I learned how to bargain for the best price at a very early age."

"You mean you really are interested in this place?"

"Let's see what the agent comes up with first," Sara said with a worried look. "My loan at the bank has already been approved, although I suspect Gabe had something to do with that. And even though I've saved almost every penny Gabe's paid me over the past six months, my finances are still strained. It'll be expensive getting a business off the ground. And I'll have to think about furniture, too. Both for the bakery and for upstairs."

"Leave the furniture to me," Betsy said. "When Joe's folks died a few years ago, we stored more furniture than I care to think about in my attic and out in the barn. With a little elbow grease, we'll have this place looking so *quaint,* all of those rich folks from Vail and Aspen will think they've traveled back in time to the Old, Old West."

Sara smiled. "What would I ever do without you?"

"Don't worry," Betsy teased, "I have an ulterior motive in making myself so useful."

"And what would that be?"

"Let's just say I expect a huge discount on all the pastry my heart desires."

"You've got yourself a deal," Sara agreed as Karen swept back in, giving Sara the thumbs-up sign.

"Well, it looks like you're in business." Betsy beamed.

Sara let out a long sigh. "Yes, I guess it does."

But her excitement was overshadowed by two major concerns. One, spending every nickel she had on a business that could easily fail. And her second was knowing once she committed to leasing the property, there was no turning back on her and Gabe.

"Are you really sure you want to do this, Sara? Going out on your own is a big step. Shouldn't you stay at the ranch and try to work things out with Gabe?"

"Going out on my own is the only way I *can* work things out with Gabe, Betsy."

"And does Gabe understand this?"

Sara shook her head. "Of course not. He thinks I'm leaving because I'm not sure how I feel about him."

When Betsy didn't comment, Sara asked, "Is that what you think, too, Betsy?"

Betsy sent her a sympathetic look. "I believe you love Gabe, Sara. But Gabe's a black-and-white kind of guy. You either love him or you don't. No in between. No if you do this, I'll do that. If you leave the ranch, there's a big chance you could lose him. I just want to make sure you understand that."

"I do understand that," Sara said. "But I'd rather lose Gabe completely than spend the rest of my life wondering if Gabe only settled for loving me because it was best for Ben."

And before she lost her nerve, Sara walked across the room where the real estate agent was holding out a pen so Sara could sign the lease on the big chance she was willing to take.

"WELL, I SURE HOPE you're happy."

Gabe stopped cleaning out the stall and turned to find Smitty standing behind him, leaning on his cane. "Happy about what?"

"About letting Sara walk out of your life," Smitty said. "She just told me she's signed a lease on the old Blake house in town."

Gabe frowned. “And why does that surprise you? You told me the other day Sara was planning to go look at it.”

“It surprises me, because I thought the two of you had patched things up,” Smitty said. “The past few days butter wouldn’t have melted in your mouths the way you’ve been acting around each other.”

“And you think if I act like a jerk and refuse to talk to Sara, she would change her mind and want to stick around?”

“No. But I think if you march into that house right now and tell Sara you love her, it might put an end to this foolishness.”

Gabe tossed the pitchfork aside and faced Smitty with his hands at his waist. “I’ve already tried that approach, remember? It wasn’t good enough for her. Leave it alone, old man. It’s over between us.”

Smitty didn’t leave it alone. “What are you saying, Gabe? That you don’t love Sara enough to ask her to stay?”

“Maybe I love Sara enough to let her go.”

“Well, that’s just plain bullshit.” Smitty hobbled off.

Gabe picked up his pitchfork and went back to work.

So. It really was final.

Sara was still determined to leave.

And he was still determined to let her go.

SARA HAD BEEN so busy cleaning her new place from top to bottom, and hauling furniture from the Grahams' over the past few weeks, Christmas had sneaked up on her like a thief in the night. She stood alone in the darkened den, mesmerized by the twinkling lights on the giant fir tree, and finding it hard to believe it was already Christmas Eve.

One more day then she and Ben would move to Redstone.

Sara reached out and touched one of the slender branches, thinking back to the day Gabe had asked her to go with him and Ben in search of the tree. It had been such a glorious December day—the sunshine turned the heavy snow into a blanket of sparkling white glitter, the sky above them so clear and blue it took her breath away. It had also been the only day she'd spent any time with Gabe since the night Ronnie strolled through the door and changed the course of their lives.

On the way up the mountain, they'd stopped to make a snowman in the middle of the forest, adorning the chubby character they created with a variety of bells and cones covered with wild bird seed as a Christmas present for their feathered neighbors. Ben had instigated a fierce snowball fight, which Gabe eventually won, despite the fact that she and Ben had teamed up against him.

It was Ben who had first spotted the tree farther up the slope where Gabe had taken them. Watching Gabe's patience with Ben—holding the ax but allowing Ben to help cut the tree—had only deepened Sara's love for him.

Gabe loved Ben unconditionally.

Sara would never doubt that.

Too bad he didn't feel the same way about her.

In fact, Gabe had become a stranger to her. He'd been pleasant enough, but guarded. He'd made sure there were no chance touches between them. No brushing of their shoulders. And not once had he sent her a meaningful glance, offering her even a glimmer of hope that he still loved her.

They'd reverted to the initial roles they'd played when she first moved to the ranch, as if the intimate moments in each other's arms had never happened. At times, Sara wondered if their brief love affair had only been a figment of her imagination.

"Sara."

She turned to see Gabe standing right behind her.

He handed her one of the cups he was holding. "I thought you might like some more hot cider." He looked at the tree, rocking back on his heels before clearing his throat. "I wanted to talk to you alone before tomorrow morning."

Sara issued a silent prayer that Gabe was going to ask her to stay. Yet in her heart she knew he'd already allowed things to progress too far if he'd had any doubts about her leaving.

"You're right," she said. "Things are going to be pretty hectic in the morning. I can't decide who's more excited—Smitty or Ben."

"Yeah," he said, glancing at the parcels around the tree. "It's been a long time since we had any reason to have a tree or presents around here."

Sara winced at his comment. But dammit, she wasn't going to cry!

She sat on the floor in front of the tree.

Gabe surprised her by sitting beside her.

On impulse, Sara reached out and grabbed a brightly wrapped package. "This is for you," she told him. "From me."

He hesitated for a moment, but took the package. He tore off the shiny silver paper, opened the lid then lifted out the expensive pair of leather chaps from the box. The look in his eyes immediately softened. "You obviously knew how much I needed these," he said. "Thank you."

He surprised her again with a quick kiss on the cheek. Then he pulled an envelope from his shirt pocket.

"I didn't wrap your present in fancy paper," he said, "but Merry Christmas, Sara."

Sara opened the envelope and looked inside to find three neatly folded documents. Removing the first one, she leaned closer to the tree lights to read it. She gasped when she realized she was holding the deed to the Blake house.

"Gabe—"

"I offered you money once for the wrong reason. Let me give you something now for the right reason. Those landmongers in Aspen would have raised the rent on your next lease the minute your bakery started showing any profit. That deed will keep the profit in your pocket."

Sara still willed herself not to cry. She couldn't pull it off.

When she took the second document from the envelope, Gabe said, "I bought the Jeep for you when you came to the ranch and I want you to keep it. That's the title. And that's another thing I won't argue about."

Reaching up, Sara swiped at her cheeks. She took the final document out of the envelope.

But before she could unfold it, Gabe pulled her to him for a long, final kiss. When he released her, Sara didn't miss the moisture in his eyes.

"Be happy, Sara. You deserve it."

Then Gabe was gone.

And Sara was left sitting by the Christmas tree alone, staring at the papers that would put an official end to Gabe and Sara Coulter's marriage of *in*convenience in ninety short days.

CHAPTER TWENTY-THREE

FRESH FROM THE OVEN officially opened for business the third weekend in January, which coincided with the annual Sled Dog Races. Everyone in town agreed Sara couldn't have picked a more perfect time to launch her new business.

People from all over the country made the trip to join in the festivities. It was a big business weekend for the whole town of Redstone. And to Sara's delight, her new establishment became an instant hit with everyone who walked through the bakery's front door.

"Please tell me we can call it a day," Betsy pleaded on Sunday evening. "It's officially six o'clock, my feet are killing me and I vote we lock up."

Sara took the keys from her apron pocket and tossed them to Betsy. "You lock up, I'll bring coffee."

She turned back to the pile of dirty baking pans stacked in the sink and actually smiled. She'd been so busy during the last day of the dog races that, other than a few lonely blueberry muffins left in the pastry case, everything had been sold out.

Dirty dishes or not, it had been a good day.

By the time Betsy locked the front door, Sara was holding two cups of coffee. She shooed Betsy over to one of the tables in the front room.

As the snooty real estate agent had envisioned, a variety of rustic tables and chairs now provided more than enough atmosphere for jet-setting tourists in search of a quaint Old West bakery. Betsy's shabby-chic decorating ideas couldn't have been more perfect. An assortment of antique cooking utensils adorned the newly-painted walls—rolling pins, biscuit cutters, even a wooden-handled mixer.

Another of Betsy's contributions had been from her greenhouse. Large clay pots filled with bright-faced pansies were everywhere, perking up the room.

"What we need now is a fairy godmother who will have that kitchen cleaned up by the time we finish our coffee." Betsy heaved a sigh of relief when she flopped onto one chair and propped her feet up on another.

"You've already been my fairy godmother," Sara told her. "I never would have survived this weekend without your help, Betsy. Thanks for ignoring my offer to send you home where you belonged."

Betsy shrugged off the compliment. "This wasn't my first dogsled weekend. I knew it would be a madhouse in town. I just never expected people to be lined up on the sidewalk waiting to get inside a bakery."

Sara grinned. "I think people really were impressed with the pastry, don't you?"

"Impressed? Are you kidding? I saw two little old ladies rolling around on the ground fighting over a piece of your baklava."

Sara laughed. "I realize this is not going to be my typical business weekend, but I did have several different business owners from Glenwood Springs approach me about supplying them with fresh pastries every week."

"That could really be a lifeline," Betsy agreed. "If you cater to a few of the big hotels and restaurants, you could build up a steady clientele."

Sara took a sip. "I'm just not sure how I could swing it this soon, Betsy. I can't keep imposing on you, and I'm not in the position to hire someone to look after the bakery while I make deliveries to Glenwood Springs every week."

"Then recruit a deliveryman," Betsy said with a twinkle in her eye. "You know. Someone who would love to ride over to Glenwood Springs once a week and get caught up on all the juicy gossip in the county."

"You mean Smitty?"

"I can't think of anyone better suited for the job."

"And wouldn't Gabe just love that? Smitty's already spent more time here than he has at the ranch over the past few weeks helping us pull things together. I can only imagine what Gabe would do if he found out I'd recruited Smitty."

Betsy shrugged. "You never know. After all, Gabe did drop by for a minute yesterday."

"Only to pick up Ben and take him to the dog races."

"Yeah, but he did stop by. Maybe Gabe will turn out to be more supportive about your move to town than you think."

Sara took another sip. She wasn't pinning any false hopes on Betsy's assessment of the situation. Gabe had stopped by at the absolute busiest part of her day, and he'd stayed only long enough to collect Ben and offer a brief nod in her direction. It had been Smitty, not Gabe, who had brought Ben back later that night.

What Sara also hadn't told Betsy was that Gabe had turned her down both times she'd asked him over for supper shortly after she and Ben had moved to town. She'd wanted him to see her in a different light. Wanted him to realize she was a smart, resourceful woman perfectly capable of running her own business and supporting her son—and not the charity case she'd been when Gabe first met her.

But he hadn't given her that chance.

Instead, both times he'd come up with some lame excuse about being tied up at the ranch. He'd also shown no interest whatsoever in what she'd been able to do with the living quarters upstairs. On the two occasions he *had* stopped by for Ben, Gabe had managed an exceedingly quick exit. Sara had a sickening feeling things weren't going to change anytime soon.

"Mom?" Ben yelled down from the top of the stairs. "Me and Junior's hungry."

"Junior and I," Sara yelled back.

"Can you bake us a pizza, Mom?"

Sara looked over at Betsy.

Betsy looked back at Sara.

"Oh, no, he didn't," Betsy said. "Please tell me that child did not have the audacity to even utter the word *bake* to you."

Sara laughed.

Betsy narrowed her eyes. "Shall *you* go up and strangle him, or shall *I?*"

"You go strangle him," Sara said. "I'll put a pizza in the oven."

"No, I'll spare his life this time," Betsy said. "But only because the boys have been such angels to stay upstairs and play all afternoon."

"Did you hear me, Mom?"

"We heard you," Betsy responded. "You want pizza."

"Fresh from the oven," Sara quipped.

She pulled her weary self up from her chair and headed for her less than tidy kitchen.

GABE FROWNED at the pitiful group gathered around his dining room table. "Would you guys stop acting like Smitty just served you a plate of poison? I remember a time when you inhaled anything he put in front of you."

"Yeah, but that was before Sara spoiled us with all her good cooking," Slim muttered.

"Yeah," another hand spoke up. "I'd kill for a big plate of Sara's meat loaf and that homemade gravy of hers about now."

"Things sure ain't the same around here without her," Smitty chimed in. "And that's a fact."

Gabe slammed his fist on the table.

Every paper plate fluttered when he did.

"Do you think it might be possible to get through at least one meal without someone moaning and groaning because Sara is gone?"

Gabe pushed his chair back from the table. And stormed out of the room.

He grabbed his jacket from the coatrack next to the kitchen door, left the house and headed for the barn. He was as frustrated over the whole situation as the rest of them. But most of all, he was angry with himself for taking that frustration out on Smitty and the boys.

Dammit!

Didn't they realize they weren't the only ones who missed Sara. His heart ached every time he looked across the table and saw her vacant chair.

Gabe stomped into the barn and walked toward Bruiser, who immediately trotted to the front of his stall, bobbing his head up and down for Gabe's attention. "At least you don't try to make me feel guilty about Sara leaving," Gabe told the horse as he rubbed Bruiser's nose.

Bruiser nuzzled against his hand, and Gabe reached into a feed bag hanging by the stall for a handful of oats.

"What do they expect me to do?" Gabe asked when Bruiser began lapping up the oats. "Run to Redstone every night with a bouquet of flowers and a box of chocolates in hand? Don't they realize I gave it my best shot when Sara was living right here under my own roof, and that wasn't good enough for her?"

Bruiser snorted in agreement with Gabe's tirade. He got another handful of oats for his loyalty.

"And all this calling me up and inviting me over for supper. What's that about? Doesn't Sara realize it tears my heart out to be in the same room with her? That it's everything I can do to keep my hands out of her hair? Doesn't she have any idea that I love her more than I ever thought I could love anyone or anything else in the world?"

Bruiser gave Gabe's shoulder a sympathetic nudge.

In return, Gabe patted the big horse's neck and rubbed him affectionately between the ears. "You and I have the type of relationship I can understand," Gabe told the horse. "I take good care of you, and you don't doubt my intentions. You don't second-guess my motives. You instinctively know that you can always depend on me. And that's the way a relationship should be. Just like the one I have with you."

He gave Bruiser a final pat, walked to the barn door and looked out at the silver snowcapped mountains illuminated by the moonlight. He'd been worried from the beginning that Sara might have trouble settling into a solitary life on the ranch. And when he thought about it, he couldn't really blame her for preferring town—even one as small as Redstone—to the isolation that surrounded them at the Crested-C.

It took a special kind of woman to live on a ranch and cook three meals a day for a bunch of hungry men. And although Sara had never once complained about her chores, he hadn't missed the excited glow on Sara's face Friday when he'd stopped by the bakery to pick Ben up for the dogsled races.

Surrounded by the crowd of the people crammed into the bakery, Sara looked happier than he'd ever seen her. And although he couldn't help but feel more than a little jealous, in his heart, Gabe was pleased.

Sara had started her new life, and from every indication it would be a huge success. It was time now to get his own life back on track and stop grieving for what might have been.

Gabe closed the barn door, ready to apologize for the tantrum he'd thrown earlier. Smitty and his ranch hands had stood by him through the good times and the bad.

And accepting life without Sara, Gabe knew, was going to be an extremely bad time for many more months to come.

CHAPTER TWENTY-FOUR

SARA KEPT the bakery closed on Sundays. She needed at least one day set aside for Ben. They'd also started attending church with the Grahams. She was waiting for Gabe to bring Ben home now. Gabe had promised to have Ben back by eight so he wouldn't miss Sunday school at ten.

She hurried to her bedroom window when she heard the truck stop out front. Then Sara flew back to her dresser for a final look in the mirror before she went downstairs. Pushing a few stray hairs into her hair clip, she couldn't help thinking that it would serve Gabe right if she took the clip out altogether.

But she'd never do that.

Taking her hair down was special to Gabe.

He considered it sensual—and private.

By the time Sara reached the door, Gabe and Ben were already walking up the steps. Ben bolted into the room with the gusto of a soon-to-be six-year-old, slipped off his backpack and thrust it in Sara's direction.

"Hi, Mom," he said as Sara bent down for a kiss. "I had a great time. Some of the boys came up to the house last night and played music. And every time Smitty blew his old harmonica, Bandit howled like this." Ben threw his head back. "Woo-woo. Wooooooooooooooo."

Sara laughed and helped Ben off with his coat before she smiled at Gabe. "Would you like a piece of pie and some coffee, Gabe?"

He was still standing on the porch. And the look on his face said he wasn't coming in.

"Better not," he said, patting his stomach. "I've dropped a few pounds eating Smitty's cooking. I'd like to keep it that way."

If his comment was meant to hurt her, it worked.

But Sara wasn't ready to give up yet. "Just coffee, then?"

Gabe shuffled from one foot to the other.

Ben reached out and grabbed his uncle's hand. "Come on in, Uncle Gabe. I want you to see my bedroom."

Removing his Stetson, Gabe stepped inside the door and allowed Ben to pull him across the room to the stairs. When the two of them started to the upper level, Sara followed. But she held back when they reached Ben's bedroom, leaning against doorjamb instead of entering the room herself.

"I guess my room's okay, but it's not as good as my room at home," Ben announced, producing, Sara noticed, a slight smile from his uncle at the knowledge that Ben still considered the ranch *home.*

"Well, I think this is a great room, Ben," Gabe said as he inspected some of the drawings Ben had taped on the wall beside his bed.

"That's Bess and Bandit," Ben said proudly, pointing to two shapes that slightly resembled man's best friend. "And that's Lightning," he informed Gabe, pointing to a rather legible drawing of a white pony.

"What about this one?" Gabe asked.

"That's you and Smitty sitting on the corral fence."

"Is my nose really that big?" Gabe teased.

Ben giggled.

"Gabe," Sara interrupted, "if you change your mind about something to eat or drink, I'll be downstairs."

"No thanks, Sara. I really need to get going."

He said it without even turning to look at her.

He swung Ben high into the air, then he dropped Ben feetfirst onto the bed.

"Excuse me?" Sara said before she could stop herself.

"Uncle Gabe lets me jump on the bed sometimes when I stay over," Ben quickly explained.

"Troublemaker," Gabe whispered behind his hand.

Ben giggled again and gave his uncle a final hug.

Sara moved out of the doorway when Gabe walked in her direction. "Thanks for letting Ben spend the weekend with you, Gabe."

"Thanks for letting him come," Gabe said.

He started down the hallway. But when he disappeared down the stairs, Sara hurried after him before she lost her nerve. "Gabe, wait."

He turned at the bottom of the stairs. "You got the final annulment papers, right?"

Sara nodded and started down the steps. She'd cried all day when she got them. During the three long months since she'd left the ranch, she'd tried everything possible to keep the channels of communication open between them. She'd extended invitations he never accepted. She'd stopped by the ranch on numerous occasions to leave baskets of goodies for him and the boys. She'd even swallowed her pride, like she was doing now, begging for his attention.

Nothing had worked.

And Sara had finally come to the end of her rope.

By the time she came to a stop on the last step,

tears she couldn't hold back were streaming down her face. "I've lost you, haven't I, Gabe?"

He frowned at her question. "Don't do this, Sara. It's too hard on both of us."

Sara reached out to touch his arm.

He moved out of reach.

"Don't, Sara," he said again.

He walked out her front door and never looked back.

Sara whispered, "Goodbye, Gabe."

He'd answered her question.

She'd lost him—forever.

DURING THE WEEKS that followed her final plea to Gabe, Sara was forced to accept the fact that her decision to leave the ranch had been the right choice. Gabe had made it clear he wanted nothing to do with her. All he'd ever cared about was Ben. And since she wasn't putting any restrictions on letting Gabe see Ben whenever he wanted, he had no use for her at all.

Sara no longer called extending invitations he wouldn't accept. Nor did she take time out of her busy schedule and drop by the ranch to get a glimpse of him. She didn't even hover in the doorway on those Sundays when Gabe brought Ben back to town, hoping he would stay and visit. Instead, a casual wave from the porch when Gabe drove up with Ben was the extent of any face-to-face contact between them.

Just like today, Sara thought as Ben bounced up the steps alone while Gabe pulled away from the curb and drove off down the street. Ben had called her early that morning, begging to skip church so he could be at the ranch when a new foal was born.

"The baby foal is so cute, Mom," Ben said. "I named him Starfighter. He has a white star on his forehead."

He only grimaced a little when Sara gave him a hug. Her little boy was growing up fast.

"Are you hungry?" Sara asked as Ben dumped his gear inside the door.

"I'm real hungry, Mom. Me and Smitty worked real hard. We had to hold Matilda's head while Uncle Gabe helped her birth her baby."

"Smitty and I," Sara corrected, thinking back to Gabe's concern that the Crested-C wouldn't mean anything to Ben unless he grew up on the land. Her son might not be living at the ranch at the moment, but Sara had a new understanding of what it meant to be blood kin.

The Crested-C meant everything to Ben.

"The snow's melting real fast now, Mom," Ben said as they walked into the kitchen. "Can we go home soon?"

His question broke her heart.

Hoping to avoid the subject until she could figure out exactly what to say, Sara said, "So how hungry are you, sweetie? Hungry enough for a big cheeseburger?"

"With extra, extra cheese."

Later, after Ben was occupied with his extra, extra cheeseburger, Sara took a seat beside him. "You know, Ben, I'm not sure we'll be moving back to the ranch anytime soon."

Ben stopped chewing and gave Sara a concerned look. "You mean 'cause you and Uncle Gabe got nulled?"

Sara raised an eyebrow. "Where did you hear that?"

"Junior said you and Uncle Gabe got nulled. What's *nulled,* Mom? Does it hurt?"

More than you'll ever know.

"The word is *annulled,* Ben. It's a legal term for what happens when you end an agreement. Uncle Gabe and I agreed to stay married for six months. Our six months were over, so we ended our agreement."

Ben thought it over and said, "Junior said I didn't have a family anymore. But when I asked Uncle Gabe about it, he said we'd always be a family, no matter what."

His words turned Sara inside out.

"Your Uncle Gabe was right. You're a Coulter, remember? And whether you live at the ranch or in town, you'll always be a Coulter and Gabe will always be your family."

Ben swiped away his milk mustache with the back of his hand. "Are you still a Coulter, too, Mom?"

Sara shook her head. "No, honey. I'm not a Coulter anymore."

She almost added, *I never really was.*

"Uncle Gabe said when school's out you might let me stay at the ranch longer than just on weekends so I can learn to take care of Starfighter all by myself." He sent her a pleading look. "Would you, Mom?"

"We'll see," Sara answered.

Ben smiled.

The words slipped right out of Sara's mouth. "Did your Uncle Gabe say anything else about me?"

"Like what, Mom?" Ben asked innocently.

"Forget it, honey, it isn't important," Sara said, immediately ashamed of herself for tying to pump her own son for information about a man who didn't love her.

"Uncle Gabe did say something about you this morning."

Sara held her breath.

"He said—" and Ben mimicked Gabe's deep

voice "—you'd better get out of that mud puddle, Ben, or your mom will skin both of us alive."

Sara sent Ben a pretend mean look and said, "And I will skin you both alive, young man, the day you come home looking like you've been playing in the pigsty."

Ben giggled at Sara's response.

Sara left Ben to finish his cheeseburger. But her heart was filled with an incredible sadness. It was over between her and Gabe. The sooner she accepted that fact the better. One day Gabe Coulter would look just as good driving away from her house as he did driving up to the curb.

Comforted by that lie, Sara headed for the kitchen to check on the orders Smitty would deliver to Glenwood Springs tomorrow morning. Against her better judgment, Smitty had assumed the role of her deliveryman, though it had been Betsy, not Sara, who had recruited him for the job. As Betsy predicted, Smitty had jumped at the chance to make a weekly trip out of Redstone so he could broaden his horizons in the gossip arena.

Smitty's assurance that it was none of Gabe's business, however, didn't qualm Sara's concern that Gabe disapproved of Smitty's new job. And if she hadn't needed Smitty's help so desperately, she would have vetoed the idea from the very beginning.

But her catering orders had actually put her over

the top as far as her finances were concerned. And although the bakery had done much better than she originally hoped, the catering income would make it possible for her to pay off her loan at the bank sooner than she expected.

As soon as the loan was paid off, she intended to start making mortgage payments to Gabe. And that was something she wasn't going to argue about.

Satisfied her orders were complete, Sara heard Ben's footsteps on the stairs, then waited until the music from his favorite video game filtered down from his bedroom. Ben being home had put an end to the deadly silence that often consumed Sara. But even Ben's presence on Sunday evenings didn't lift Sara's blue mood.

Sunday evenings had once been private time with Gabe.

Of course, Betsy reminded Sara on a regular basis that her solitary life was her own choosing. And that she owed it to herself to accept some of the offers she'd received from the good-looking cowboys who made a special trip to the bakery to have an excuse to talk to her.

"Give Gabe a run for his money," Betsy had urged Sara time and again. "Let Gabe know he'd better come to his senses before someone else takes his place."

In time, maybe Sara would date someone else.

And comforted by that lie, too, Sara cleared Ben's plate from the table, placed the dishes in her industrial dishwasher and switched off the kitchen light. She wandered upstairs and, after making a quick check on Ben, Sara seated herself on the sofa in the spare bedroom she'd turned into a den.

Absently flipping through the television channels, she stopped when she found one of her favorite programs: *From Eats to Sweets with Don Inglehorn.* The famous food critic lived in Denver, but he traveled nationwide. And his viewers had the privilege of tagging along with him as Don toured the country looking for the best restaurants, bistros and bakeries to review.

"Next month in May," Don Inglewood said smiling into the camera, "I'll be visiting one of my favorite places in my home state of Colorado. And you can count on me to be looking for the best Glenwood Springs has to offer—from eats to sweets."

Sara was so excited she could hardly contain herself.

She grabbed the portable phone sitting on the end table beside her and hit Speed Dial. "You aren't going to believe this," Sara breathed into the phone, "but I just heard on television that Don Inglehorn is going to be in Glenwood Springs next month."

"Don who?"

"The famous food critic, Betsy! How hard do you think it would be to find out where he'll be staying in Glenwood Springs?"

"Oh. My. God." Betsy gasped. "Please tell me this guy is so hot you've forgotten you even know Gabe Coulter."

Sara laughed. "Sorry to disappoint you. Don is in his fifties and he's obviously gay. But I want a basket filled with goodies from Fresh from the Oven waiting for him when he arrives at his hotel."

"Well, I guess we could call around and ask."

"You'll help me find out where he's staying then?"

"Oh, pooh," Betsy said. "What a silly question."

CHAPTER TWENTY-FIVE

SMITTY SAT perched on the back of the flatbed truck late Thursday afternoon while Gabe wrestled with a bale of barbed wire that was currently getting the better of him. It irked Gabe every time the old man jammed his hand into a bag of doughnuts that had Fresh from the Oven written in bright pink letters across the front of the bag.

"Did you hear that big food critic from Denver is going to bring his television crew to Redstone next month and give Sara an exclusive interview on his program?"

Gabe stiffened at the sound of Sara's name. But he went back to work unraveling the length of wire he needed from the bale.

"Yeah," Smitty said, "it seems this Don Inglehorn makes a trip once a year to the Hotel Denver over in Glenwood Springs for a mineral bath in that natural hot springs pool they have. The guy had such a fit over Sara's marble pound cake last week he drove straight to Redstone and asked Sara to be on his television program."

"Maybe he'll want to interview her damn deliveryman, too," Gabe grumbled, and gave the fence post a sound thud with head of his mallet.

"The whole town's excited over the exposure Redstone's gonna get," Smitty rambled on. "The mayor's arranging a big celebration while the camera crew's in town. He's gonna block off Redstone Boulevard and have an old-fashioned square dance. Everyone agrees we need to do all we can to promote Redstone with the whole nation watching."

Gabe sent Smitty a mean look. "Would you stop yapping and bring me those wire cutters?"

Smitty abandoned his doughnuts, slid off the back of the truck and hobbled over to Gabe with the wire cutters in his hand. Gabe cut the wire. But when he drew back to give the fence post a final hit, Smitty said, "I heard those cowboys who hang around the bakery are already fighting over who's gonna take Sara to the dance."

The mallet landed on Gabe's left thumb.

"Dammit!" he cursed, and dropped the mallet.

Smitty leaned over and looked at the ugly gash. "That's gotta hurt, Gabe. And that's a fact."

Gabe stuck his thumb into his mouth. The look he sent Smitty was lethal.

Smitty only grinned. "There's some duct tape in the glove box of the truck. Want me to get a piece and bandage your thumb?"

"I'll get it my damn self," Gabe fumed. "And maybe if I put a piece of duct tape over your mouth we might get a little work done around here."

Gabe stomped off toward the cab of the truck.

But he wasn't smarting from his injured thumb nearly as much as the sound of Smitty's satisfied chuckle over being able to get him riled up.

"Like I give a damn who takes Sara to the dance," Gabe mumbled as he used his teeth to tear off a piece of the silver tape. "Sara can square-dance down Redstone Boulevard naked for all I care."

Gabe folded the tape gently over his thumb.

"But she won't find me standing on the sidelines watching her do it," Gabe vowed. "And that *is* a damn fact."

"Did you say something, Gabe?" Smitty called out.

Gabe kicked the door shut with the heel of his boot. When he stomped around the truck, Smitty was still standing beside the bale of wire, a mocking grin on his whiskered face.

"I said if you'd put forth as much effort being a ranch foreman as you did delivering doughnuts, we might finish repairing this fence before dark."

"Yeah, that's what I thought you said." Smitty kept grinning at him.

"YOU LOOK SO PRETTY in that red dress with your dark hair and brown eyes, Sara," Hazel Cooper said on Friday afternoon. "Marge showed me the material you picked out for the pioneer dress she's making you. And now I understand exactly why you picked that gingham print. Red is definitely your best color. And you're going to look gorgeous in your television interview. I just can't tell you how pleased the mayor is that everyone is willing to dress in Old West costumes for the square dance while Don Inglehorn's in town. Don's program is broadcast coast to coast, you know. And we'll be bringing a taste of the Old West right into living rooms all across the nation. Why, the mayor said he wouldn't be surprised if our tourist business more than doubles by the end of the summer."

Sara smiled when Hazel finally completed her run-on sentences. The mayor's wife was a robust woman, always impeccably dressed like the mayor was himself, and Hazel always referred to her husband as *the mayor* since she and her dearly beloved were the only two people in Redstone impressed with his title. Hazel could also tell you who'd been in town on any given day, and what time of day they arrived and what time they left.

Sara just wished Hazel would hurry up.

Thirty minutes of endless chatter was enough. Plus, it was Friday and she had to get Ben's clothes ready to go to the ranch for the weekend. Gabe wouldn't arrive until later, after Ben got home from school, but the bakery had been so busy all morning she was running way behind schedule. And the last thing Sara wanted was to give Gabe the impression she'd delayed packing Ben's things on purpose in order to have an excuse to talk to him.

Those days were long gone and Sara intended to keep it that way.

Hazel finally pointed to the bakery case. "And I'll take a dozen of those scrumptious blueberry tarts. They're the mayor's favorite, you know. And that's something you might want to mention in your interview, Sara. I don't know if you realize it or not, but it's amazing how much influence political figures have over the public. I read once that after President Jimmy Carter mentioned he ate a certain brand of cereal for breakfast, sales for that brand increased fifty percent."

"You don't say," Sara mumbled as she plopped the last of the blueberry tarts into the bag with the doughnuts, the apple turnovers and the cream puffs, and handed it across the counter. After giving the woman her change, Sara smiled and said, "Tell the mayor I hope he enjoys these."

"Oh, the mayor always enjoys anything I bring him from your bakery, Sara. In fact—"

The incessant babbling suddenly stopped.

Sara looked up as Ronnie Kincaid walked into the bakery.

Hazel sent an anxious look at Sara, but she smiled when Ronnie walked up beside her. "Why, I was just telling the mayor the other day that you hadn't been to town in ages, Ronnie."

Ronnie sent her a bored look. "And you would know, wouldn't you, Hazel?"

Hazel's face flushed. "Well!" she huffed. "What a positively *rude* thing to say!"

Hazel marched out the door.

Ronnie turned her attention to Sara. "I didn't want an audience for what I came to say."

Sara straightened her shoulders. "Then you were rude to Hazel for no reason. I'm not interested in anything you have to say, Ronnie."

"Too bad. We need to talk about Gabe."

"Gabe and I are over."

Ronnie laughed. "Don't insult me. We both know it won't be over for Gabe until you and your brat leave Redstone."

Sara's hackles rose at the nasty reference about Ben. But a glance at the bakery's front window reminded Sara she needed to say calm. At least half of the other shop owners and a dozen or more locals were already sending nervous glances in their direction. In the midst of it all was the mayor's wife chattering at the top of her lungs.

"My *son* and I aren't going anywhere," Sara said, looking back at Ronnie. "And I think you should leave before you draw a larger crowd than the one standing outside there now."

Ronnie sent a brief glance over her shoulder. She sneered at Sara when she turned around. "Do you really think those idiots out there give a damn about you? Because they don't. They've all been waiting to see me kick your ass since the day you brought Billy Coulter's bastard home to Redstone."

Sara paled and felt the closest she'd ever come to slapping anyone.

"Your insults aren't going to work on me, Ronnie. If I let you bully me into a fistfight like some common tramp, those people out there will assume everything they've ever thought about me behind my back is true. But I'm not like that. And you're not worth me looking cheap now."

Sara stepped around from behind the counter. "I'll show you your way out." She walked over to open the front door.

"Sara, look out!" someone screamed.

Sara turned around in time to see a chair sailing through the air. It missed her completely. But it hit the bakery's plate-glass window with a thunderous bang.

Glass exploded in every direction.

The crowd outside scattered like a flock of pigeons.

RONNIE WALKED calmly out of the bakery and down the front steps. She ignored the angry stares and the nasty insults people hurled in her direction and continued across the street to her Suburban. Her next stop would be to the pay phone at Jones Country Store. Then she was headed to Crested Butte where she intended to give Charlie Biggs a huge piece of her mind.

"Stupid people," Ronnie mumbled a few minutes later as she hopped out of the Suburban and headed for the phone booth.

And she was talking about Gabe, Sara and Charlie.

She'd tried to wait them all out for six long months. She'd waited for Gabe and Sara to patch things up on their own. And she'd waited for Charlie to get his head out of his ass and come home to the Flying-K where he belonged.

But she wasn't waiting any longer.

Not after she'd heard through the cowboy

grapevine that Charlie was drinking his life away in Crested Butte where some little blond barmaid had her eye on him. *And* not after she heard some big-shot food critic was coming to interview Sara at her bakery next month.

Gabe might be a fool, but Ronnie wasn't.

If she hadn't caused that scene in the bakery, she and Gabe would have ended up all alone playing solitaire like her father, while Charlie settled down with the blonde and Sara moved off to Denver to be the idiot host on some worthless television baking show.

Sliding behind the wheel again, Ronnie headed for Crested Butte, pleased with herself whether anyone else appreciated what she'd done for Gabe and Sara or not. Not that she'd ever admit she'd only caused a scene so Gabe would come running to Sara's rescue. Let everyone rush to console poor, sweet little Sara after big, bad Ronnie threw a chair through her window. The whole town could think whatever they wanted.

But Ronnie would tell Charlie the truth.

He'd told her not to come looking for him until she patched things up between Gabe and his wife. Ronnie intended to remind Charlie that he didn't say a damn thing about being nice and polite when she did it.

EVERYONE HAD RUSHED toward Sara the minute Ronnie drove away. And thirty minutes later when Sara looked around, it appeared half of Redstone was still crowded into the bakery to assess the damage and offer help.

"Don't worry about that window, Sara," Hank assured her. He turned to the man standing beside him. "Right, Harve?"

The owner of the hardware store nodded. "We'll all pitch in and put some plastic over your window," Harvey Miller said. "And I'll order the new glass first thing in the morning."

Someone else handed Sara a glass of water that she eagerly accepted. She had just taken a long sip from the glass when the mayor's wife hurried inside.

"I just talked to the mayor," Hazel said, slightly out of breath, "and he insists that you press charges, Sara. Ronnie's been nothing but trouble from the day she was born, and—"

"No," Sara said, stopping the woman's prattle mid-sentence. "I appreciate everyone's concern, but I don't intend to keep a feud going by pressing charges against Ronnie. She and I had a disagreement. It's over. And I intend to keep it that way."

When the crowd began to break up, Sara heard someone say, "Sara's a better person than I am."

"Me, too," someone else agreed. "I'd have me a lawyer before the sun went down."

After the bakery finally emptied, Sara let out a long sigh. She'd known Ronnie would force a showdown sooner or later. She was just thankful Ronnie had decided to do it while Ben was at school. One more week and school would have been out for the summer and Ben would have heard every ugly thing Ronnie said about him.

Even the thought made Sara shudder.

She headed to the kitchen for a dustpan and broom. She couldn't help but think about something else Ronnie had said—that it wouldn't be over for Gabe until Sara left Redstone. It made her wonder if maybe she should leave so both of them could finally get on with their lives.

She had just knelt down to sweep up the jagged pieces when she heard another set of heavy footsteps on her front porch steps. When Sara looked up Gabe was standing in the doorway, his face as white as the Stetson hat he always wore.

"Are you okay?"

It was all Sara could do to keep from running straight into his arms. Instead, she said, "I'm fine," and went back to sweeping the glass into the dustpan.

He removed his hat and took a step in her direction. "Someone called the ranch and said Ronnie took out your front window with a shotgun."

Sara stood up. "You know how people in this town like to exaggerate. Ronnie had her say. She threw a chair through my window. And that's the end of it."

Sara turned and headed into the kitchen.

Gabe followed, hat in hand.

Sara ignored him and dumped the glass into the trash. But when she turned around he was standing way too close for comfort. Only inches were left between them.

He placed his hat on her kitchen counter, looked at her and said, "I know I've been a real jerk, Sara—"

"Don't, Gabe," Sara told him, fighting back the tears. "Like you told me once, it's too hard on both of us."

Sara tried to push past him.

But Gabe grabbed her hands, forcing her to stay.

"Just hear me out," he begged. "Please."

Sara wanted to tell him no. That she wasn't interested in anything he had to say. Just like she had that first day she met him.

But in spite of everything, Sara still loved him.

"I came to make sure you weren't hurt," he said, still holding both of her hands. "But I also stayed up all night rehearsing what I wanted to say to you when I came for Ben tonight. The stunt Ronnie pulled got me here a little sooner."

Gabe dropped down on one knee.

"I love you, Sara. You're the most important thing in my life and I can't live without you. I want you to wear my mother's wedding dress. I want you to ride up *our* driveway in a horse-drawn carriage filled with roses. And I want the whole town standing on *our* front lawn when I ask you to be mine forever. Just say I'm not too late. Say you still love me and that you'll marry me."

Sara pulled Gabe up and threw her arms around his neck.

Gabe hugged her against him. "Is that a yes?"

The long kiss Sara gave him answered his question.

Gabe kissed her again.

And again.

Until more footsteps echoed through the bakery.

Ben ran into the kitchen at full speed. "Wow, Mom. What happened to the front window?" But he looked even more surprised when he saw Gabe. "What are you doing here already, Uncle Gabe?"

Gabe put his arm around Sara and pulled her close.

"Hey!" Ben protested. "And why are you guys doing all that mushy stuff today?"

"We're doing all the mushy stuff," Gabe said with a big grin, "because your mom just agreed to marry me."

"Forever this time?" Ben asked.

Gabe looked at Sara for an answer.

"Forever this time," Sara said.

Ben didn't hesitate. He ran and jumped into Gabe's outstretched arms. "Can we go home now, Mom?"

Sara looked at Gabe for an answer.

"Not until after the wedding, Ben," Gabe said, and smiled at Sara. "I have some wooing to do first."

"Wooing like Bandit does?" Ben threw his head back. "Woooooooooooooooooo."

Sara and Gabe both laughed.

But Sara knew her fairy-tale romance was finally about to begin.

RONNIE DROVE down the main street of Crested Butte and slowed to a stop when she saw Charlie's truck parked in front of a bar called McAdoo's. She parked the Suburban three doors down and took her time walking up the sidewalk.

If she found Charlie all hugged up with the blonde, Ronnie wouldn't be responsible for her actions. But if she didn't, she intended for Charlie to be with her when she left Crested Butte.

She took a deep breath and walked into the bar. She breathed a sigh of relief after her eyes adjusted to the dim lighting. Charlie was sitting at the bar. Alone. But Ronnie's eyes narrowed when the perky little blonde behind the bar suddenly sidled over and practically pushed her boobs in Charlie's face.

Ronnie marched across the room and slid onto the stool beside him. The deadly look she gave the blonde sent the bimbo skittering off to the far end of the bar to attend to another customer. Charlie, however, refused to even acknowledge Ronnie's presence.

She looked over at him and said, "Some cushy job you must have if you're drinking this early in the day."

"I'm between jobs at the moment."

Ronnie reached over, picked up the glass of whiskey sitting in front of him and drained every drop. "I still need a foreman at the Flying-K."

"That's your problem," he said, and signaled to the blonde. "Jack on the rocks again, sweetheart."

The blonde sent Charlie a go-to-hell look.

"Boo-hoo," Ronnie mocked. "Sweetheart looks pissed."

Still, Charlie ignored her.

He also ignored the blonde when she slammed his drink down a few minutes later. He reached for his drink, his eyes still focused straight ahead. "What are you doing here, Ronnie?"

Ronnie shrugged. "Well, you told me not to come looking for you until I patched things up with Gabe and his wife. I did that earlier today. So here I am."

"Right," he said, and brought the glass to his lips.

"Of course, I had to cause a scene in town so Gabe would have reason to come running to the rescue. I threw a chair through the bitch's window at her bakery."

Charlie sputtered in his drink.

"But you know me," Ronnie said, and sighed. "That's just the type of woman I am. Bold. Brassy. Always hard to handle."

Charlie lowered his glass to the bar.

"Yeah," Ronnie said, "you never know what to expect from a woman like me. But you can guarantee one thing. The sex will always be sizzling and leave you begging for more."

Charlie looked at her for the first time. But it wasn't lust Ronnie saw in his eyes. Charlie loved her—he always had. And what he needed now was to hear her say out loud that she felt the same way about him.

"I love you, Charlie. I want you to come home."

Charlie grinned. "All you had to do was ask, babe."

CHAPTER TWENTY-SIX

SARA STOOD in Betsy's upstairs guest bedroom, admiring Mary's wedding dress in the full-length mirror. Like the picture of Mary on her wedding day, Sara wasn't wearing a veil. Instead, Betsy had entwined a sprinkle of baby's breath through her dark, upswept hair. Sara touched the delicate lace across the bodice, wondering if her own daughter-in-law would want to wear this dress one day.

Or possibly a daughter—if she and Gabe decided to have children. They'd agreed not to make that decision until later, after they'd had a chance to enjoy being a real husband and wife.

The bedroom door opened and Sara turned. She smiled when Betsy, Annie and Dessie filed into the room.

"You look beautiful, Sara," Dessie said.

"Absolutely perfect," Betsy agreed.

"Breathtaking," Annie said, tossing her long,

blond hair over one shoulder and looking pretty breathtaking herself in the pale pink dress she was wearing.

Annie would be her maid of honor. And Smitty, of course, would be Gabe's best man. Ben would do his part by walking Sara down the aisle and giving his mother away.

Sara held her arms out.

They all came together for a group hug.

"Having my three best friends here is what makes everything perfect," Sara told them. "Each of you has been there for me through some of the most difficult times in my life. I can never thank you enough for that."

"And now we're here for the most wonderful time in your life," Betsy said. She looked down at her watch. "But if we don't get moving Smitty is going to kill me. I promised him I'd have the bride to the ranch on time."

"That Smitty sure is a bossy old cuss," Dessie said.

"And that's a fact," Sara and Betsy said in unison.

Everyone laughed.

"Your dress qualifies as something old, Sara," Annie said. She reached out and fastened a pearl bracelet around Sara's wrist. "This is something new from me."

"Annie, it's beautiful," Sara gushed.

"And I brought you something borrowed," Dessie said. "When you told me your dress was Victorian, I knew this would be perfect. It belonged to my great-grandmother."

Sara's eyes filled with tears as Dessie pinned a pink and ivory cameo brooch on the delicate lace at her throat. "I'll take good care of it today, Dessie."

"And did you remember your something blue?"

Sara answered Betsy's question by pulling up the hem of the dress to display the lacy blue garter Betsy had bought for her.

"Then let's go get married," Betsy chirped happily.

As they started down the stairs, Dessie said, "I'm so glad you aren't going to give up your bakery, Sara. Married or not, a woman needs a little independence."

As they started out the door, Sara said, "I have Betsy to thank for keeping the bakery. If she hadn't agreed to become my partner, running the bakery and taking care of things at the ranch would have been too much."

"Oh, pooh," Betsy said. "The town never would have forgiven me if I'd let Sara close the bakery. Fresh from the Oven put Redstone on the map after Sara's big TV interview. Tourists make a beeline for it the minute they hit town."

As they headed toward Sara's Jeep, Annie said, "And to think all of this started because of me and my big mouth."

"Now wait just a minute," Dessie said. "I was the one who told Sara she should come to Colorado with Gabe."

Annie and Dessie were still arguing over who was responsible for Sara's new life when they got into the Cherokee. But Sara knew the truth. Gabe was responsible for her being on the way to her wedding. Over the past three months Gabe had wined her and dined her and wooed her until she often felt silly for making such a request.

But she deserved it.

Sara could say that now and truly believe it.

GABE STOOD beneath the arched trellis the florist had set up on his front lawn, trying to pretend standing in front of the entire town didn't make him nervous. He was the first one to see the carriage top the hill and start down the long driveway leading up to the house.

Smitty was at the reins in his Sunday best. And the woman Gabe loved, more beautiful than he'd ever seen her, was sitting in the carriage, wearing his mother's wedding dress and surrounded by a sea of pink and white roses.

His heart was so full, Gabe feared it might burst.

He loved Sara more than life itself. And over the past six months he'd realized how wrong he'd been about what it meant to be married and in love. Love and marriage wasn't some fifty-fifty deal where you only had to contribute your half to make the relationship work. Love and marriage demanded one hundred percent of everything you had to give one hundred percent of the time. And Gabe intended to give Sara one hundred percent each and every day for the rest of their lives.

"Here comes the bride," someone shouted.

Everyone stood.

And Gabe stood a little straighter. A big smile spread across his face when his bride's carriage rolled to a stop.

Sara waved and blew him a kiss.

"I NOW PRONOUNCE you—" the pastor stopped when Ben suddenly left his place between Gabe and Sara and motioned for the man to bend down.

Whispers skipped across the waiting crowd.

When the pastor straightened, he winked at Ben and said, "I now pronounce you husband and wife *forever* this time."

Everybody clapped and cheered.

"You may now kiss the bride."

This time, Gabe did kiss his bride—thoroughly.

Sara couldn't have been happier as she took Gabe's arm and walked down the long aisle between the two sections of folding chairs lining their front lawn. Ben ran on ahead. Eager, Sara knew, to show Junior the large feast waiting behind the house and, of course, the wedding cake.

But she felt Gabe stiffen when they reached the last row of chairs. He whispered, "What's *she* doing here?"

Sara pulled him along until they were far enough ahead of the crowd following not to be overheard. "I invited Ronnie and Charlie to the wedding," Sara confessed. "In fact, I delivered the invitation to the Flying-K in person."

Gabe laughed. "Only to gloat, I hope."

"Maybe just a little," Sara admitted. "But no one in town has spoken to Ronnie since the day she broke my window. I wanted to put an end to that nonsense. I know what it's like to be the outsider, Gabe. I wouldn't wish that on anyone. Not even Ronnie."

Gabe pulled her to a stop, the expression on his face filled with more love than Sara had ever seen. "I love you, do you know that?"

"Yes," Sara said, "and I'll never doubt it again."

She was a Coulter.

At last, she was home.

* * * * *

Celebrate 60 years of pure reading pleasure with Harlequin!

To commemorate the event, Harlequin Intrigue® is thrilled to invite you to the wedding of The Colby Agency's J. T. Baxley and his bride, Eve Mattson.

That is, of course, if J.T. can find the woman who left him at the altar. Considering he's a private investigator for one of the top agencies in the country—the best of the best—that shouldn't be a problem. The real setback is that his bride isn't who she appears to be…and her mysterious past has put them both in danger.

Enjoy an exclusive glimpse of Debra Webb's latest addition to
THE COLBY AGENCY:
ELITE RECONNAISSANCE DIVISION

THE BRIDE'S SECRETS
Available August 2009
from Harlequin Intrigue®.

The dark figures on the dock were still firing. The bullets cutting through the surface of the water without the warning boom of shots told Eve they were using silencers.

That was to her benefit. Silencers decreased the accuracy of every shot and lessened the range.

She grabbed for the rocks. Scrambled through the darkness. Bumped her knee on a boulder. Cursed.

Burrowing into the waist-deep grass, she kept low and crawled forward. Faster. Pushed harder. Needed as much distance as possible.

Shots pinged on the rocks.

J.T. scrambled alongside her.

He was breathing hard.

They had to stay close to the ground until they reached the next row of warehouses. Even though she was relatively certain they were out of range at this point, she wasn't taking any risks. And she wasn't slowing down.

J.T. had to keep up.

The splat of a bullet hitting the ground next to Eve had her rolling left. Maybe they weren't completely out of range.

She bumped J.T. He grunted.

His injured arm. Dammit. She could apologize later.

Half a dozen more yards.

Almost in the clear.

As she reached the cover of the alley between the first two warehouses she tensed.

Silence.

No pings or splats.

She glanced back at the dock. Deserted.

Time to run.

Her car was parked another block down.

Pushing to her feet, she sprinted forward. The wet bag dragged at her shoulder. She ignored it.

By the time she reached the lot where her car was parked, she had dug the keys from her pocket and hit the fob. Six seconds later she was behind the wheel. She hit the ignition as J.T. collapsed into the passenger seat. Tires squealed as she spun out of the slot.

"What the hell did you do to me?"

From the corner of her eye she watched him shake his head in an attempt to clear it.

He would be pissed when she told him about the tranquilizer.

She'd needed him cooperative until she formulated a plan. A drug-induced state of unconsciousness had been the fastest and most efficient method to ensure his continued solidarity.

"I can't really talk right now." Eve weaved into the right lane as the street widened to four lanes. What she needed was traffic. It was Saturday night—shouldn't be that difficult to find as soon as they were out of the old warehouse district.

A glance in the rearview mirror warned that their unwanted company had caught up.

Sensing her tension, J.T. turned to peer over his left shoulder.

"I hope you have a plan B."

She shot him a look. "There's always plan G." Then she pulled the Glock out of her waistband.

Cutting the steering wheel left, she slid between two vehicles. Another veer to the right and she'd put several cars between hers and the enemy.

She was betting they wouldn't pull out the firepower in the open like this, but a girl could never be too sure when it came to an unknown enemy.

Deep blending was the way to go.

Two traffic lights ahead the marquis of a movie theater provided exactly the opportunity she was looking for.

The digital numbers on the dash indicated it was just past midnight. Perfect timing. The late movie would be purging its audience into the crowd of teenagers who liked hanging out in the parking lot.

She took a hard right onto the property that sported a twelve-screen theater, numerous fast-food hot spots and a chain superstore. Speeding across the lot, she selected a lane of parking slots. Pulling in as close to the theater entrance as possible, she shut off the engine and reached for her door.

"Let's go."

Thankfully he didn't argue.

Rounding the hood of her car, she shoved the Glock into her bag, then wrapped her arm around J.T.'s and merged into the crowd.

With her free hand she finger-combed her long hair. It was soaked, as were her clothes. The kids she bumped into noticed, gave her death-ray glares.

They just didn't know.

As she and J.T. moved in closer to the building, she grabbed a baseball cap from an innocent bystander. The crowd made it easy. The kid who owned the cap had made it even easier by stuffing the cap bill-first into his waistband at the small of his back.

Pushing through the loitering crowd, she made her way to the side of the building next to the main entrance. She pushed J.T. against the wall and dropped her bag to the ground. Peeled off her tee and let it fall.

His gaze instantly zeroed in on her breasts, where the cami she wore had glued to her skin like an extra layer. A zing of desire shot through her veins.

Not the time.

With a flick of her wrist she twisted her hair up and clamped the cap atop the blonde mass.

"They're coming," J.T. muttered as he gazed at some point beyond her.

"Yeah, I know." She planted her palms against the wall on either side of him and leaned in. "Keep your eyes open. Let me know when they're inside."

Then she planted her lips on his.

* * * * *

Will J.T. and Eve be caught in the moment?
Or will Eve get the chance
to reveal all of her secrets?
Find out in
THE BRIDE'S SECRETS
by Debra Webb.
Available August 2009
from Harlequin Intrigue®.

HARLEQUIN®

INTRIGUE®

BREATHTAKING ROMANTIC SUSPENSE

Shared dangers and passions lead to electrifying romance and heart-stopping suspense!

Every month, you'll meet six new heroes who are guaranteed to make your spine tingle and your pulse pound. With them you'll enter into the exciting world of Harlequin Intrigue— where your life is on the line and so is your heart!

THAT'S INTRIGUE— ROMANTIC SUSPENSE AT ITS BEST!

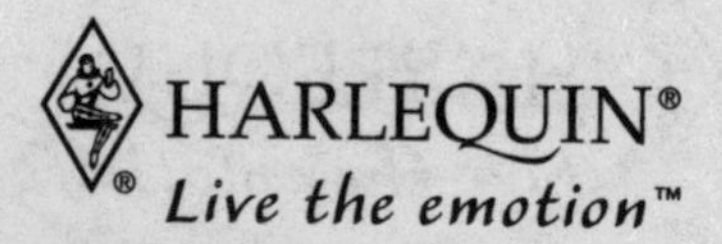

www.eHarlequin.com

INTDIR06